I0542274

Marked Men

ACCEPTABLE BEHAVIOR

JENNA BYRNES

Acceptable Behavior
ISBN # 978-1-78430-992-3
©Copyright Jenna Byrnes 2016
Cover Art by Posh Gosh ©Copyright January 2016
Interior text design by Claire Siemaszkiewicz
Pride Publishing

This is a work of fiction. All characters, places and events are from the author's imagination and should not be confused with fact. Any resemblance to persons, living or dead, events or places is purely coincidental.

All rights reserved. No part of this publication may be reproduced in any material form, whether by printing, photocopying, scanning or otherwise without the written permission of the publisher, Pride Publishing.

Applications should be addressed in the first instance, in writing, to Pride Publishing. Unauthorised or restricted acts in relation to this publication may result in civil proceedings and/or criminal prosecution.

The author and illustrator have asserted their respective rights under the Copyright Designs and Patents Acts 1988 (as amended) to be identified as the author of this book and illustrator of the artwork.

Published in 2016 by Pride Publishing, Newland House, The Point, Weaver Road, Lincoln, LN6 3QN, United Kingdom.

No part of this book may be reproduced, scanned, or distributed in any printed or electronic form without permission. Please do not participate in or encourage piracy of copyrighted materials in violation of the authors' rights. Purchase only authorised copies.

Pride Publishing is a subsidiary of Totally Entwined Group Limited.

If you purchased this book without a cover you should be aware that this book is stolen property. It was reported as "unsold and destroyed" to the publisher and neither the author nor the publisher has received any payment for this "stripped book".

Pride Publishing books by Jenna Byrnes:

Second Time Around
Carnal Collision
Night Shift
Stroke of Luck
Practice Makes Perfect

Marked Men
Acceptable Behavior

Cattle Valley
Truth or Dare
Fool's Gold

Kansas City Heat Volume One
Dixon's Duty
Peyton's Pursuit

Kansas City Heat Volume Two
Cameron's Code
Taylor's Task

Kansas City Heat Volume Three
Gage's Gift
Rainey's Release

Kansas City Heat Volume Four
VanDoren's Vice
Hyatt's Hunt

Rose and Thorn Society Volume One
Switching Seth
Brooklyn Bound

Rose and Thorn Society Volume Two
Never Say Never
An Unexpected Win

Anthologies
Lasso Lovin': Fortune's Way

Hard Riders: Clear Blue Sky
Aim High: Search and Rescue

Collections
My Secret Valentine: Secret Rendezvous
Frostbite: Night Fall

ACCEPTABLE
BEHAVIOR

Dedication

To J., even though you never could get that first tattoo!

Chapter One

"Ouch, that hurts!" The child jerked his arm away and looked up with an irritated expression on his face.

Dr. Travis Nelson released his grip on the boy and ruffled the youngster's hair. "Sorry, champ. Looks like you have a broken arm." He turned to the child's mother. "The X-ray shows it's a slight fracture, but it'll heal better in a cast. I'm going to have the nurse call over to the orthopedics office and see when they can work you in. We'll give you the films to hand carry. Hang tight here for a few minutes."

"Thank you." The relieved woman smiled at him gratefully, then batted her eyelashes. "I really appreciate it. The other moms on the playground were right. You're the best." She crinkled her nose.

"Don't mention it." He opened the door and motioned for his nurse to follow him out. Travis looked at the boy one more time. "Sit tight here for a bit, Jason. Nurse Izzie will be back with some instructions for your mom, and we'll see if she can't find a toy for you."

"Thank you." The child offered a small smile in return.

Travis pulled the door closed behind his nurse, Isabelle.

Izzie made a note on the paper chart then grinned up at him. "Four out of five moms on the playground recommend Dr. Travis to heal their child's boo-boos."

He blinked at her, a serious expression on his face. "Only four out of five? What happened to the fifth one?"

"She's gay." Izzie shrugged. "Can't win 'em all."

He laughed. "Yeah, well, maybe if we put the word out that I am, too, I wouldn't feel like I had to take you along for protection every room I went into."

"Nah." She shook her head. "We might lose too much business. Let the moms keep their fantasies. It's our job security."

"Whatever. Get Jason an appointment with the ortho guys, will you, please? Copies of the X-rays for his mom to take along. And a toy."

Izzie scanned her notes. "Ortho, X-rays, toy. Check. Janel's in room two with your next patient."

"Check." He smiled at her then went to the next exam room, pausing to wash his hands just before he entered. He grabbed the chart and examined it quickly. Levi Madison was a six-year-old male with fever, ear drainage and loss of appetite. *Ear infection.* The nurse had pegged it. He just needed to confirm the diagnosis.

He opened the door and went in. A thin boy with curly blond hair sat on the exam table. "Hi, Levi. I'm Dr. Travis. I hear you're not feeling well today."

The boy shook his head.

"Well, we're going to have a look and see if we can't get you fixed right up." He turned to the chairs next to the table and was surprised to see a man rather than a woman accompanying the child.

And what a man! He sported the same curly blond hair as the child, just long enough to cover his ears and collar. His eyes were clear blue, and there was a small tuft of hair below his bottom lip. *A soul patch.* Travis tried not to focus on the lips, but they were as pink and perfect as any he'd ever seen.

When he rose, Travis could see that the guy was an incredible specimen. About the same height as Travis, this guy's physique displayed firm muscles in his arms and flat abs covered by a thin T-shirt. He wore tight, faded jeans that were ripped in several places. Travis thought—he *thought*—that he could see the outline of a large cock running down the inside of one thigh through denims. He could have drooled, but he had enough professionalism to control himself. "Mr. Madison? I'm Dr. Travis Nelson."

"Sam Madison," he confirmed and extended his hand.

Travis grasped it and shook. The hunk's grip was warm and strong, not clammy or weak. *Of course it is.* What else would he have expected from a man that fine? *Focus, Doc.* He cleared his throat. "So, how long has Levi been running a fever?"

"A couple of days, I guess. His mom didn't say for sure. But it's not getting any better, and now he doesn't have an appetite. He says his throat isn't sore."

Travis nodded. *His mom didn't say for sure. Does that mean Dad doesn't live with Mom?* His mind wandered, conjuring up scenarios. They all led to the same conclusion. If Sam had a child and the mom was still in the picture, he was more than likely not gay. *Too bad.*

He sighed. *Ah, well. Doctors need fantasies, too.* He pulled an otoscope from his pocket and turned to Levi. "Let's have a look in those ears." He inspected both ears and found them inflamed with drainage. Travis listened to the boy's breathing, checked his mouth and assessed the vital signs on the chart. "Well, this doesn't look too bad." He glanced in the ears one last time and spoke to the nurse. "Otitis media."

"Yes, Doctor." Janel made her notes in the chart. "You want amoxicillin?"

He turned back to the father. "Any antibiotic allergies?"

The handsome man looked confused for a moment. He looked at Levi. "You're not allergic to any medicines, are you?"

Levi shook his head.

Sam glanced at Travis and shrugged. "I guess not."

Travis hesitated, uncertain about taking the word of the child. *If I had a kid, I sure as hell would know if he had a drug allergy.* "You're not sure? Has he had many ear infections?"

"I don't think so." Sam looked at Levi again. "Do you get sick like this often?"

"No," Levi answered.

Hmm. Travis wondered if Sam was a 'weekend dad'. They saw that pretty often on Fridays. He turned to the boy. "Have you taken antibiotics before? The kind I'm considering is pink, and you take it by mouth three times a day."

"The pink stuff." Levi nodded. "Tastes like bubblegum."

"That's right, the pink stuff." Travis gazed back at Sam. "If you don't know his history, I'd feel better if we had access to records from his last pediatrician."

Sam appeared uncomfortable. "Honestly, Doc, I don't think he's ever had one before. His mom's always just taken him to the free clinic or the County Health Department for shots. I know he's had those—he had to be up to date when he started school."

"True." Travis felt a little better knowing at least that much. He couldn't help but ask, "Does he have insurance?"

The father shook his head.

"Okay, well, listen. I'm going to write you a prescription for amoxicillin. Take it to any pharmacy. This stuff is cheap, like, four bucks. It has to be refrigerated, and he has to have it three times a day. If you can get it filled this afternoon, give him two doses today, and start again in the morning, three times a day. Continue until it's gone. Don't stop once he's feeling better. Can you do that?"

Sam set his jaw. "I'm pretty sure I can master the concept of three times a day, yeah."

The jab hit Travis where it was intended, and he smiled. "I'm sorry, I didn't mean to offend. Some parents — most, in fact — don't get how important this is. They never get around to finishing all the medicine once the child is up and running around again." He scribbled instructions onto his prescription pad, tore the top sheet off, and handed it to Sam.

Accepting the paper, Sam smiled back. "No offense taken. I'm definitely not like most parents. But this little guy means the world to me, so I'll make sure he gets the pink stuff three times a day until it's gone. I promise you that."

Travis nodded. "Good enough. Nurse Janel, here, is going to give you some information on treating the symptoms of otitis media. Some tips and tricks to making the patient feel better. And then she's going to find a toy for Levi." He leaned down to the boy. "You've got to promise to take your medicine like a trooper and do what your parents ask you to do, so you can get all better. Can you do that?"

Levi nodded.

"Good man." Travis rose and faced Sam. "He should feel better in a day or two. If he's not himself in a week, call the office and we'll see him again."

"Thank you, Dr. Travis." Sam's voice had an amused tone.

He grinned and, with a slight nod, walked out. Sam seemed to be mocking him just a bit, but he didn't care. It wasn't his idea for the doctors in their practice to be called by their first names — 'Dr. Travis' versus 'Dr. Nelson', as most physicians who saw adults were called. The men who'd started the pediatric practice had wanted it that way. He was merely the newest partner hired on as the others aged toward retirement. And he didn't mind good-natured teasing. It did sound strange to call himself Dr. Travis, but whatever. He'd graduated medical school with honors and had chosen pediatrics as his specialty. People could say what they wanted, or think what they wanted. *I'm a good doctor who cares about children.* That was what kept him going during the day.

* * * *

His other passion was what kept him going at night. Travis opened the garage door to his house and went to his Specialized Tarmac Mid Compact bicycle. The beautiful black, red and silver frame called to him. He could have had the worst day, or the best day, it didn't matter. When he arrived home, he wanted only one thing. He'd change into riding clothes, drink a protein shake, and head out for a ride. Depending on his route, he could ride twenty-five to thirty miles in an evening. On the weekends he'd ridden one hundred miles before, but usually averaged somewhere around fifty.

He managed twenty-five and called it good for the warm spring evening. He'd agreed to participate in a road race for the Chicago Children's Charity Fund on Sunday morning, so he didn't want to overdo it the next couple of days. Travis enjoyed philanthropic events, but tried not to be too vocal about it. He'd learned early on that none of his partners were quite as physically fit as he was, and they were quick to volunteer him to represent the practice during athletic challenges. He didn't really mind. The very image of kindly old Dr. Webster trying to get astride a bicycle of any kind always brought a smile to his face.

Back home again, he wiped down his bike with soft rags before heading inside to the shower to tend to himself. A hard ride always worked up a good sweat, and today was no exception.

Travis closed the shower door and stood under the tepid water spray. He reached up and switched the showerhead to a pulsing massage beat and allowed it to work on his back for a few minutes. When he finally went for the soap, he realized his cock was standing at half-mast and the realization surprised him. *When was the last time I had a hard ride that didn't involve my bike?* He couldn't remember back that far.

His last serious lover had moved on well over a year ago. He and Jack had been together for three years, but had slowly grown apart. A pharmaceutical rep, Jack had spent his days on the road and had gotten to the point where he hadn't wanted to do much of anything at all in the evenings, except drink. He'd enjoyed his before-dinner cocktails, his dinner-time cocktails, and his after-dinner cocktails long into the evening. When Travis had expressed concern, Jack had said he could quit drinking whenever he wanted. He'd simply never wanted to. Jack had moved on to someone who wanted to drink with him, not nag him about it.

It had taken some time, but Travis had finally gotten over the split. Acceptance didn't come without some damage to his heart, though. He'd vowed to think twice before getting so deep into a relationship that he'd fall in love again. Love was for suckers. Love was for co-dependents who couldn't stand to be alone. Travis was neither of those things.

He was happy by himself, working hard, playing hard, pushing his body to its physical limits on a daily basis. He was still paying for medical school, but was finally making enough that he'd purchased a nice house and a bike that cost more than some people's first car. He was happy with the life he'd built. He was just plain happy.

Yet here he was, cock now at full attention, yearning for the one thing Travis hadn't quite figured out yet. *Okay, so I'm not completely happy.*

Adjusting the water temperature to the verge of hot, he then lathered his shaft from base to tip before returning the soap to the dish. With one hand pressed against the tiled wall and the other stroking himself, he closed his eyes to conjure up his dream guy. A muscular, athletic man with rock-hard abs and pecs he could bounce a quarter off. A man with curly blond hair and a soul patch beneath his bottom, fleshy pink lip.

Travis' eyes popped open. *Where the hell did that come from?* He'd enjoyed lots of fantasies in his thirty years, but never once had the parent of a patient tripped his trigger the way Sam Madison had today. Sam was an impressive hunk of flesh, if what Travis had seen through the faded jeans was accurate. Well hung or not, Sam was damned cute and — *what the hell?* Definite fantasy material.

Stroking his cock, he imagined unbuttoning those tight jeans and lowering them to the floor. Would he find boxers or briefs underneath? *To his delight, Travis found no underwear to fight his way through, just a long, pinkish colored shaft with a slightly purple, bulbous head. He kneeled in awe of the magnificent organ and sucked the crown into his mouth.*

Sam wanted more — needed more — and thrust his hips, sending several inches of throbbing flesh down Travis' throat.

Travis could barely breathe but he didn't care. He licked and sucked with abandon, taking all he could get into his mouth and inching forward for more.

His own cock shuddered before release overtook him, and he sprayed seed against the shower wall. He fisted his shaft and pumped for as long as he was able, until he could barely remain standing.

The shower stall was full of steam so he turned down the water temperature and washed the wall before cleaning himself. His closely cropped brown hair required very little shampoo and conditioner, but he applied each dutifully. When he felt sufficiently clean and content, he shut off the water, opened the door then grabbed his oversized towel.

Travis stepped onto the soft bathroom throw rug and proceeded to dry himself off. He was finally getting hungry, and had a nice, thick-cut T-bone steak in the fridge that he could throw on the grill and have ready in twenty minutes, along with a fresh salad.

The mirror was foggy from his overheated shower so Travis took the blow dryer and cleared it. He studied his reflection and wondered how he'd look to a man he might get naked with for the first time. Tattoos covered his body from both wrists to shoulders, his pecs, abs, back, and both legs, groin to ankle.

Travis smiled. The tats made him feel like Clark Kent, hiding a secret identity under his suit and tie. His only unmarked skin, besides his face and neck, were his hands, feet and the area covered by his briefs. He wasn't afraid to get his ass tattooed, he just hadn't done it yet. But no one, artist or not, would touch his cock with a needle. He was obsessed, admittedly, but he wasn't a fucking lunatic.

* * * *

Sam Madison grabbed the sack from the drugstore and turned to look at Levi in the back seat of Sam's Volkswagen Beetle. "Here we are. Come on, let's go see if Mom's awake."

Levi scrambled out of his seatbelt and booster seat, and slipped out of the door next to Sam. He was halfway up the sidewalk before Sam had locked the car and fallen into step behind him. He had to hand it to the boy — no matter how crummy he felt, the thought of seeing his mom perked him up like nothing else could.

They reached apartment twelve in the run-down, motel-style building and Sam unlocked the door. The stench of burnt food hit him immediately. Hurrying to the kitchen, he was relieved to see there hadn't been a fire or any serious damage done. Just a saucepan with what appeared to be macaroni boiled dry and blackened across the bottom of the pan.

Melanie was sprawled across the sofa with one eye open.

Levi went right to her and curled up in her lap.

She opened both eyes and tried to focus on him. "Hey, little man. How was school?" She ran her fingers through his hair absently.

"He wasn't at school," Sam reminded her loudly. "We've been at the doctor's office. He's got an ear infection, and has to take antibiotics three times a day."

She waved Sam off. "Fricking doctors, they're in bed with the drug companies. First reaction is always to put someone on meds. Solve the world's problems with a little pill."

Sam pulled the bottle of pink medicine and a separate dropper from the bag. He read the label then shook the bottle and drew the proper dose into the dispenser. He went to the sofa and held the medicine in front of Levi's mouth. "Open up."

Levi did, and Sam squirted the medicine in his mouth. He watched the boy swallow, then looked at Melanie. "Isn't that what you're trying to do, too? What are you on, Mel?"

"What are you talking about? I just woke up."

"Right, sure you did. You waitress at the bar from nine to three a.m. You should be able to come home, sleep while he's at school, and be awake when he gets back."

She yawned and tossed her long blonde hair over one shoulder. "You know I have trouble falling asleep."

"I know you have troubles, that's the only thing I know for sure." He stomped back to the kitchen and refrigerated the medicine, then rinsed out the dropper. "It's Friday night, don't you have to work?"

"I called in sick," she admitted.

He sighed then put the burnt pan in the sink to soak. Sam figured it would be a lost cause. Tomorrow he'd probably have to throw it away.

Sam glanced around the kitchen. It was a mess, with crumbs on the counter and table. "I've asked you not to leave food out like this. We just got rid of the bugs. We don't want to get them back."

"Sorry. I was hungry." She yawned again.

He looked at her. "Did you eat?"

Melanie thought about it. "I don't think so. I was going to make some macaroni and cheese."

"I can see you didn't eat that. What's for dinner, Mel? What's Levi supposed to eat?"

"I'm not hungry," the boy piped up, still nestled against his mother.

Sam opened one cabinet after another and finally came up with two boxes of Velveeta Shells and Cheese. *Perfect, because there's no need to add milk or butter, neither of which the fridge contains.* He found another pan and started water to boil. "You've got to eat something, Levi. This isn't the most balanced dinner but it won't hurt for one night."

He pulled three bowls from the cabinet and almost laughed when he thought about what he'd said. *One night? Was he seriously trying to fool himself that Mel and Levi ate better other nights?* They may have once, but, lately, her life was spiraling out of control and he was damned if he could figure out how to stop it.

"Need to go pee." Levi climbed down and went into the bathroom, closing the door behind him.

Sam took the opportunity to light into Mel. "What the fuck are you thinking? You should have taken him to the doctor. The guy was asking me questions and I had no idea what the answers were."

"You managed. It doesn't matter. We'll never see that doctor again."

He frowned. The doctor had been really nice, and cute as hell. Sam wouldn't mind seeing him again, himself. *Pipe dreams.* It'd been so long since he'd had a date, he was ogling anything in trousers. Especially now, with the living situation he found himself in. Circumstances were less than ideal. "Can't you think about your son for a change, and not just what you want?"

She glared at him through glassy eyes. "Don't you see? I can't think about anything right now. Robby's gone. I don't want to go on without him."

Fury welled in the pit of Sam's stomach. "Fuck that stupid stoner drug pusher! He got you hooked and you're lucky he didn't get you sent to prison with him."

Mel tried to sit up but was shaking. "Don't talk about him that way! He's Levi's daddy. I loved him. I still love him."

Sam glanced at the bathroom door and back at her again. "That kid is the only thing the stupid fucker ever did right. Knowing now what a douchebag he is, I'm sick to think he was the one who kept your family together. It obviously wasn't you."

She tried to lash out at Sam but fell back into the sofa, then laughed hysterically. "You don't know anything."

"I know you'd be screwed if I said 'to hell with you' and took off. This is *not* how I expected my life to play out, Mel."

She stopped laughing and her eyes widened. "Don't say that, Sammy. Don't even joke about leaving us. I need you. We need you."

He stomped over to the bathroom door. "You okay, buddy?"

"Yeah," came the reply, then the toilet flushed.

"Wash your hands."

"I know." Water running confirmed he'd remembered.

Sam went back to Mel's side. "I'm staying because Levi needs me. You've got to get your shit together, Mel. You're my sister and I love you, but this is *not* what I need."

"I know, Sammy. I really do know. I just— It's hard. I miss him so much."

He gritted his teeth. "Rob is looking at twenty-five years in prison, Mel. There's nothing you can do for him now. You need to focus on Levi, and being the best mother possible to him."

"I don't know if I have that in me anymore. I...don't know."

Levi rejoined them and sniffed at the smell of the pasta. "Maybe I'm a little hungry."

Sam put a hand on his shoulder. "Come on. You can help me stir it up."

* * * *

Sam fed his sister and his nephew, then settled them on the sofa together watching a movie while he cleaned up the kitchen. Satisfied they were both occupied for the time being, he went into his bedroom and closed the door. His space was small but neatly organized, nothing like the rest of the place that his sister had chosen to call home.

He flipped open his laptop computer and scanned his email. As a freelance writer, he made good money and was able to set his own schedule. Unfortunately, his sister took that to mean he really didn't work, so he was available to do whatever she needed for Levi at the drop of a hat.

Sam sighed and closed his computer again. There were two jobs he could be working on, but his heart wasn't in it. He hated seeing what Mel had become, but couldn't drag her out of the funk she'd settled into.

He'd never cared for Rob Fielding but had been supportive when they'd gotten together and had Levi. The guy had worked as a motorcycle mechanic and brought in good money, enough that Mel hadn't had to work. Sam hadn't learned until after the arrest that most of Rob's money had come from drug sales. By the time he was caught up in the police sting, it was his third strike and he'd automatically been sent away with the maximum sentence. It was then Sam had learned that Mel was not only addicted, she was nearly incapable of caring for her son on her own.

With no family to support them, Sam and Mel had come up with the plan for him to move in with her and Levi. It had seemed plausible at the time. Grateful for the help, Mel had given up her bedroom to Sam, and she slept on the sofa. She got a job waiting tables at a bar five nights a week, but didn't have to leave until Levi was in bed. Sam was there all night, and if Mel wasn't awake, he took the boy to school in the morning.

Recently, he'd had to start picking him up, too. Mel was drowning. Things were going from bad to worse.

He sauntered back out to the living room and woke Levi up long enough to swallow another dose of the pink stuff. Levi did, then settled back in and closed his eyes.

Sam shut off the lights. He wasn't going to pry the kid's grip off his mother's arm and try to put him in his own bed. He let Levi sleep where he was, and went back to his room.

Pausing long enough to stick the medicine back in the fridge, he made a mental note to go to the store tomorrow.

Something has to change. If it's not going to be Mel, it'll have to be me. The thought haunted him as he tried to fall asleep, because he wasn't sure how much more he could manage. Taking Levi to the doctor today had pushed his comfort level to new heights.

It hadn't been a totally bad experience, though. Dr. Travis was the sexiest man he'd met in ages. Sam chuckled. *The poor sap probably has a wife, three kids and a minivan.* What a waste of such a fine stud.

Sam's hand slid into his boxers but there was no life to be seen. He wouldn't have minded a nice jerk-off session, with the good doctor starring in his fantasy. Bringing his exhausted cock to life sounded like way more trouble that it'd be worth. "Strike that, reverse it," he murmured, recalling the old *Willy Wonka and the Chocolate Factory* movie quote. It wasn't his cock that was exhausted. The poor thing hadn't seen any action in months. Maybe a year. *He* was flat out exhausted, worrying about his sister and the little innocent boy who hadn't asked for anything that life was dealing him. Levi had gotten a raw deal. Sam saw it as his duty to fix that, in whatever way he could. He simply hadn't figured out how to do it yet.

Chapter Two

Sam was pleased to see Levi was feeling better on Saturday. Mel was even up and alert, and they all went to the grocery store together. Sam made sure Levi took his medicine on schedule, and had him rest most of the day. When Mel went to work Saturday night, Levi was tucked into bed, sound asleep, and Sam got several hours' worth of work done.

Sunday, Levi was almost his normal self. Sam opened the boy's backpack to see what school work he might have brought home, and spotted a flier the school had sent home with the kids. There was a festival at a nearby park, some charity event with a bicycle road race, a fun run, carnival games and food vendors.

He glanced out of the window. It looked to be great weather for early spring. He wouldn't mind getting some fresh air. Mel was racked out on the couch. He'd have more trouble keeping Levi quiet than taking him out somewhere for a little fun.

Sam left a note for Mel and headed out with his nephew. The park was just a few blocks from their apartment but he didn't want to wear Levi out, so he drove them. He maneuvered into a parking stall and they walked the rest of the way, through throngs of people.

"This is so cool!" Levi enthused as runners and bike riders passed them to complete their races.

"Yeah, they have some awesome bikes."

"You have a bike, Uncle Sammy. You should have entered the race."

Sam chuckled. His bike came from a discount store and had cost less than one hundred dollars. "These guys are a little out of my league, sport."

On a stage with a podium a speaker was presenting trophies to the winners in various categories. They sauntered up to watch and Sam was stunned when the men's bike race first place prize was awarded to Travis Nelson. He'd heard the name before he could actually see the doctor. Grabbing Levi's hand, he threaded through the crowd to get closer and, hopefully, a glimpse of him.

"Well, look at that," he murmured.

Dr. Travis was wearing bike shorts and a riding shirt, but he also sported what looked almost like compression garments on his arms and legs. They were pure white, and reminded Sam of the stockings his grandfather had to wear to prevent blood clots. Intrigued, he worked them even closer yet.

"I know him," Levi chimed in. "That's my doctor."

"It sure is." Sam kept his gaze on Travis, hoping to make eye contact.

The award ceremony broke up and the winners descended from the stage.

"Dr. Travis!" Levi shouted.

Travis glanced up and the boy waved.

He looked from Levi to Sam, confused for a moment, but then he smiled. He weaved his way toward them. "Hey!"

"Hey, yourself. Congrats. That's quite an accomplishment." Sam nodded at the trophy.

"Eh, it was nothing." Travis waved the compliment off. "So what are you doing here? And how are you feeling?" he asked Levi.

"Better." The boy nodded enthusiastically.

Sam smiled. "Pink stuff, three times a day, per doctor's orders."

"Good. And have you stopped it now that he's feeling better?"

"No," Sam and Levi said in unison.

Travis laughed and they joined him.

Sam answered the earlier question, "We just came to see what was going on, maybe get some food. The kid's finally got his appetite back."

"Great to hear. I, myself, am starved. I always am after a long ride."

"You take lots of long rides?" Sam asked.

"Almost every day."

Levi added, "Uncle Sammy has a bike. I told him he should ride the race next time."

Travis' eyebrows rose. "Yes, you should, *Uncle Sammy*."

Laughing again, Sam shook his head. "My bike is a Huffy. I don't think they'd allow me in the race."

Travis glanced around. "Speaking of which, I need to get mine into my SUV. You two want to come with, then we can find something to eat?"

"Can we see your bike?" Levi asked excitedly.

"You bet. It's back behind the grandstand." He searched Sam's face. "Okay?"

Sam shrugged. "Why not?" They followed him around back where contestants had locked their bikes.

Travis removed a thick chain and padlock that he'd threaded through both tires of his bike.

"Wow!" Levi ran his hand over one of the handlebars.

"Don't touch," Sam cautioned.

Travis waved a hand. "It's okay. He's not hurting anything. Levi, can you help me get the bike to my car?"

"Sure!" Levi held one handlebar as Travis guided the bike toward the parking lot.

Sam had to ask. "You here with your family?"

"Nope, just me." Travis came to a stop behind a silver Lexus SUV.

It was Sam's turn to be impressed. "Wow," he muttered under his breath.

Travis didn't comment, just loaded his bike into the back along with his helmet, and locked the car again. "What are you hungry for? There's Mexican food, German food and a Tex-Mex place that makes amazing barbecue sandwiches. Oh, and corndogs. They have the world's best corndogs."

"Corndogs!" Levi repeated, jumping up and down.

Sam smiled. "Sounds like we've decided. I could go for some good barbecue."

Travis leaned in. "It's not just good. It's *amazing.*"

They found the vendor and ordered, then chose a table near some of Levi's friends from school. He scarfed his food and was soon playing with the other kids near the tables.

Sam and Travis ate slower, and kept their eyes on Levi as they talked.

"So," Travis began. "You never mentioned you were 'Uncle Sammy'."

Sam chuckled. "After my mother died, my sister was the only one who ever got away with calling me Sammy. Levi gets away with it because he's Levi and, well, who in their right mind would prefer being called 'Uncle Sam'?"

Travis laughed. "Good point. No, I meant that I didn't realize you were his uncle. I assumed you were his father. You never corrected the assumption."

"I was kind of panicking," Sam admitted. "I'd never taken him to the doctor before. I couldn't answer your questions, and you started looking at me funny because of it."

"That wasn't why I was looking at you funny," Travis whispered, gazing into Sam's eyes.

Flustered, Sam hurried to look back at Levi, who was still playing happily. "I, uh, didn't know you liked to ride. Of course I didn't, I barely know you. I meant, I was wondering about the garments you're wearing under your shorts and shirt. They look like the compression stockings my grandfather had to wear."

"Similar fabric," Travis agreed. "They help wick sweat away from the body and keep me cooler when riding." He leaned in. "That's my story, anyway." He peeled back one sleeve and exposed the edge of an elaborate tattoo.

"Oh!" Sam was shocked for the second time in less than two hours. "That looks interesting. How big is it?"

"They're actually a bunch of smaller tattoos put together. They pretty much cover my skin except what you can see. And a couple places you can't see." He winked.

The act zinged like an arrow straight to Sam's heart. His skin was covered with tats? Sam was dying to see them. For the first time in he didn't know how long, his cock pulsed in his jeans. "That's just…amazing. Very cool. I'd love to see more. Why do you have them covered up?"

Travis shrugged. "I'm taking it easy on the doctors I work with. They were already shocked when they found out I'm gay. If they saw my extensive body art, I'm afraid one or two of them might stroke out."

Sam's cock hardened like a boulder. "You're, um…okay. Oh, God." He scanned the kids for Levi again and tried to keep his gaze on the boy instead of the handsome hunk who was watching him intently.

Can Travis sense that I'm gay, too? Do I want to tell him? Conflicted, he decided to keep his mouth shut for the time being.

"Sorry if that was TMI," Travis added.

Sam looked at him blankly.

"Too much information."

"Oh, of course. I knew that. No, it's fine." *Now I sound like a blithering idiot.* Sam felt a sudden urge to leave, to be anywhere but within an arm's length of the sexy doctor with the deep-set brown eyes.

Travis slapped his thighs. "Change of subject. What do you do, Sam, besides take care of your nephew?"

Whew. That was an easier topic. "I write articles for websites. I'm kind of a freelancer, but I work mostly for one specific company. They send me the specifications for what they need, I write the article and submit by their deadline."

The doctor blinked. "Fascinating. I had no idea there was such a job."

Sam shrugged. "I stumbled into it, I guess you could say. The pay is great and I can set my own hours. Which is why my sister figures 'since I'm home anyway', I can take care of Levi."

"Ah, gotcha. And your sister, what's her name, and what does she do?"

As little as possible. Sam cleared the thought and instead replied, "Melanie. She's a waitress." He wouldn't mention the name of the skanky biker bar she worked at. Maybe he'd think she worked at IHOP or Denny's.

Travis nodded. "You said your mother was gone. No other family? What about your dad?"

"He wasn't around when we were growing up. I heard he died when I was about fifteen."

"I'm sorry."

Sam shrugged again. "He was just a name to us. Not even a means of support. Mom worked hard as a cleaning woman, to put Mel and me through school—we were lucky to finish high school. Neither of us went any further. Then Mom died of cancer a couple of years ago." He glanced at Levi, who was getting dirty but still seemed to be having fun.

"That's rough. I'm sorry, Sam."

He sighed. "Yeah, well, it is what it is. I don't know, maybe if Mel and I had tried college things would be different."

"Different how?" Travis' questions were probative, but his voice was gentle.

Sam didn't feel like he was being judged, so he continued to answer. "Mel hasn't made some of the best choices. I mean, Levi is great, but his father was a piece of work."

"Is he out of the picture?"

"Since he went to prison, yeah, he is. For now, anyway."

"Oh, wow. How'd he end up in prison?"

Sam inhaled then blew the breath out. "You know, that's about as much family drama as I care to share for one day. You're a great listener, though. Thanks for that, and for lunch. I intended to pay for ours."

Travis waved a hand. "No biggie. I enjoyed the company." He glanced at Levi then back at Sam. "So, you kinda got flustered when I told you I was gay, but you didn't say much."

"I wasn't flustered," Sam insisted, but deep down he knew he had been. "It's cool. To each his own."

"I guess I have to ask, then, are you…"

Sam held his breath.

Travis finished the sentence quickly. "Seeing anyone?"

Vague. Sam got the feeling that wasn't the original question Travis had wanted to ask. His heart thumped loudly in his chest and he wondered if the other man could hear it.

How do I answer that? No, but I'd love to see more of you, including those tattoos. How could he even think about starting a relationship given his current living situation? Travis probably had a place to go, but what if he didn't, or had a roommate? How embarrassing would it be to explain that he lived in a dingy rat trap with Mel and Levi? Or that he couldn't ever make plans because he was obligated to watch the boy every evening? It was simpler just to fib and let it go at that. "Yeah, kind of. She's a great girl."

"Ah, I see." Travis put up a good front but his eyes gave him away. He appeared deflated.

Sam nearly retracted his false statement but he'd be left with the same problem. Levi and Mel were his priority right now. He didn't have time for a relationship. "We should probably go. It was great visiting with you. Thanks for being so kind to Levi."

"He seems like a good kid."

"He is. When everything else is up in the air, that's the one thing I'm sure of."

Travis' brow wrinkled. "What's up in the air, Sam? I'd like to help if I could."

Sam jumped up. "You're too kind, really. Everything's fine. I just need to get the kid home so he can rest and be ready for school tomorrow. Don't want him to miss another day."

The doctor rose and nodded. "Rest is good. Of course, you know if Levi needs anything, you can call me any time. You've got my office number."

"Thank you." Sam extended a hand.

When Travis shook it, Sam felt sparks of electricity where they'd touched. *Now I'm freaking out. We have to leave, pronto.* "Bye." He hurried over to Levi and asked him to say his goodbyes, then hustled him off to the car. Sam needed to be home, away from the prying eyes and inquisitive mind of Dr. Travis Nelson. Not to mention his bulging muscles and massive tattoos. *God, I'd love to see those tats.* Maybe someday.

He sighed. *Dream on.*

* * * *

Travis couldn't get the handsome blond with the haunted eyes out of his mind. Something was up with Sam Madison, and he suspected it had to do with the little family he was so obviously trying to protect.

And for Sam to imply he *wasn't* gay? *Bullshit.* He was as gay as Travis, he'd bet his life on that fact. What straight guy, when being questioned by a queer, would reply that he 'kind of' had a girlfriend? A truly straight man would be all over himself with details about the woman, right down to her tit size. Straight men left no doubt that they were straight. He'd seen it time and time again.

Unless… Could Sam be a gay-curious straight man? Maybe he'd never tried it, but was interested. Travis would be all over that. He could help Sam with whatever reservations he might have.

But Sam would have to let him in. Right now he seemed pretty walled-up. Travis needed to think of a way to tear down the wall, even if it was brick by brick.

He drove home from the road race and cleaned up his bike, then found a spot on his bookshelf for the trophy before he hopped in the shower. Afterward, he poured himself a tall glass of ice water and sat down to make a call.

"Hi, honey! How's your day going?" His mother sounded chipper as usual.

"Hey, Mom. Good. I rode in a charity event this morning and took first place. Got my own little trophy and everything."

"Travis! Why didn't you tell us that was going on? Dad and I would have been there."

"I know, but you just got home from Aunt Mary's last night and I figured you'd be tired."

"We're never too tired to watch you win a race. Next time, *call us*."

"Yes, ma'am." Duly chastised, he changed the subject. "So how was Aunt Mary? Recovering from her knee surgery?"

"Slowly. I guess it's pretty painful at first."

"Of course it is. Soon enough she'll begin to realize that the new knee is now her *good* knee."

"Your father is still griping that you didn't go into orthopedics. He says that specialty will benefit us more in the future than pediatrics."

Travis chuckled. "Probably right, but I wouldn't meet as many hot uncles at the ortho practice."

"Hot uncles, huh? What's his name? When did you meet him?"

He hesitated. "Eh, it's too soon for that, Mom. But let's just say this one's got potential and leave it at that."

"Okay, just promise to let us know if it advances past 'potential'."

He chuckled again. "You know I will, but don't hold your breath. The guy's got issues, and I haven't quite figured out the depth and scope yet."

"What kind of issues, Trav?"

He recognized the concerned tone in her voice. He'd heard it often enough during the Jack years, so he was quick to reassure. "Nothing really bad, not like Jack. He just doesn't seem to have a lot of money. And his family is kind of messed up. No parents anymore, and I haven't figured out what's up with his sister, and why the brother was taking the kid to something as important as a doctor visit."

"Oh, yes, you are important," his mother teased. "Families do that for each other, especially when there are no grandparents in the picture. You'd know that if we had any grandchildren of our own. Sometimes the parent needs a helping hand."

"I do know that, and would you let me find a man before we have to start worrying about where the grandchildren will come from?"

"Certainly. Find-A-Surrogate.com is one place to start, though they seem rather pricey. I think you might be better off finding a woman yourself and making arrangements through a lawyer. I bet your friend Alex would help with something like that."

"Mo-ther." Travis rubbed his temple with his free hand. "I'm sure Alex could handle the paperwork because he's a very good lawyer. But you're putting the cart before the horse, *again*."

"Just saying, if you decide not to wait for a man, you know Dad and I will help you with the child, as much as we're needed. We'd love to do it."

"Thanks for that. But if I'm having trouble finding a guy when I'm single and unattached, what makes you think it'd be any easier if I was a single father? The kid would scare off half of the men I meet."

"If he's scared off, then he isn't the right man for you."

"Got it, Mom. Appreciate the input. How was your week?"

"Good. I've got most of my flowers planted. Another couple weeks and I can put in the tomatoes and cucumbers."

"That'll keep you busy."

"Not that busy, so remember to call next time you're in a race. Or just call for no reason. We miss you, Trav."

"I'm fifteen minutes away. We see each other regularly. How can you miss me?" he teased.

"Because that's what moms do, so there. Quit giving me static. And would it kill you to 'like' some of the stuff I post to your Facebook page?"

"I'm never on Facebook, Mom."

"Then maybe I should stop posting all the funny pictures and jokes."

"No, you go right ahead. I'll get on there one of these days and have myself a regular laugh riot."

"You are a rotten, ungrateful son," she teased through her chuckle.

"Top five percent of my class in med school, Mom."

"Yeah, and you remember what they call the people who graduated in the bottom five percent, don't you?"

Travis smiled. "Yeah." He and his mother both said at the same time, "Doctor."

He grew serious for a moment. "I'm not ungrateful, and that's one of the reasons I called you today. Meeting this guy reminded me of how lucky I am in many regards. *Most regards.*"

"Dad and I are lucky too, honey. Be patient with your new friend. Not everyone opens up as easily as you do to new people. He might just need some time."

Time. For some reason, the thought bugged him. "Yeah. I hope he has time. Have a good week, Mom. Love to you and Dad."

"Right back at you, son. Take care."

Travis ended the call and leaned back in his chair. Talking to his folks always helped him put things into perspective. He could give Sam some time, if he knew for sure the guy was interested in him. Right now all he had was the slim possibility of a definite maybe. And a 'kind of' girlfriend, which he still wasn't buying. He'd get to the bottom of it, one way or another.

* * * *

Travis hadn't come to any conclusions and by Thursday he'd started to feel frustrated. He needed to find a way to meet up with Sam. If they didn't talk or even see each other, Sam would never know how Travis really felt.

Hell, I'm not even sure how I really feel. He just knew he wanted to see Sam again.

"Dr. Travis, the nurse at Jefferson Elementary School called. They've had a playground accident," Janel told him at four o'clock. "She thinks it's a broken arm. They're sending the family right over."

He sighed. Clinic ended at three-thirty except for the doctor on call, which today was lucky him. "Sure. Call ortho and alert them, so they don't send everyone home. Get X-rays first thing and we'll figure out what needs to be done."

"You've got it." She hurried off to prepare a room.

Travis dictated some charts until Janel returned to his office. "The Madisons are here. You saw Levi last week for an ear infection."

His senses perked up. "He's the broken arm?"

"I'm not so sure it's broken. He'll be back from X-ray in a few minutes."

"Thanks." Travis' heart pounded and he suddenly felt guilty for wishing he could see Sam again. He'd never dreamed Levi would get hurt.

Hurrying to the X-ray department, he saw Sam and a thin woman with long blonde hair standing just outside the room where films were shot.

He stepped alongside Sam. "Hey."

The handsome man glanced at him, then relief washed over his face. "Oh, hey! I'm glad you're here. Levi's been asking if he'd get to see you."

"I'm on call today, so yep, you've got me." He glanced at the woman who'd turned to face him. His first thought had been to wonder if she was Sam's girlfriend but one look at her face answered that. She was the feminine version of Sam. "Oh, wow. Are you twins?"

Sam smiled. "Yeah. Dr. Travis, this is my sister, Melanie Madison. Mel, this is Dr. Travis Nelson."

She curled her lips into an unfriendly snarl. *"Dr. Travis.* How cute." To her brother she muttered, "I don't know why we had to come here. He's just going to send us somewhere else, and we'll have twice the bills. We should have gone straight to the ER."

Travis knew at that moment that even if Sam and his twin had been the same sex with the same haircut, he would have been able to instantly tell them apart. Sam was sweet and gentle, and knowing Mel for all of two minutes, he could already see that she had an ugly soul. Or maybe it was a damaged soul, with an ugly face on it. "Don't worry about the bill," he said to Sam. "I'll need to see the X-ray before I can determine if he needs to go elsewhere. Fractures are best treated by orthopedic specialists, but let's not get ahead of ourselves."

"Okay." Sam appeared nervous, like a good parent would be.

His sister looked bored and pissed off. "Is there somewhere I can go have a cigarette?"

Travis gazed at her levelly. "No. He'll be out in a moment, and we'll determine what's wrong with his arm. I'd assume you'd want to be here for that?"

"Whatever." She turned her back on him.

Sam looked at him sheepishly. "Sorry," he mouthed.

Travis nodded. If anything, *he* felt sorry for Sam. But knowing that Melanie was his twin made it easier to understand why Sam stayed with them.

The door opened and Janel led Levi out. The boy hugged his mother with one arm, then glanced up. "Dr. Travis!"

"Hey, buddy. You can stop by to see me anytime you want, you know. You don't have to fall off a jungle gym."

"I didn't mean to." Levi grinned.

Janel led them to an exam room.

"Right up here." Travis patted the paper-covered table, and helped Levi climb up. "I'm going to go look at the X-rays and see what we've got. I'll be right back."

As Janel followed him out, he heard Melanie say, "Hey, since this happened at school, we should be able to sue them or something, shouldn't we?"

The nurse closed the door and Travis glanced at her. She made a wide-eyed face, but neither of them said a word. He went to his office and looked at the films. He'd learned when children were involved it was best to see them first and determine the seriousness of the injury, before showing the patient and parents. Some people had a tendency to freak out when a break was bad.

Fortunately, Levi didn't have a fracture. A mild sprain, if anything. He instructed Janel to let the ortho practice know and to bring him a sling.

He returned to the exam room and as he opened the door, heard Melanie was still talking. "He's kind of cute, I guess, but you could do better."

"I like him," Levi insisted.

"It doesn't matter," Sam whispered in a hushed voice. "He's married with three kids." He stopped talking and glanced up as the door opened.

For a moment Travis thought they'd been talking about him, until he heard the part about being married with kids. Sam knew better, so they obviously weren't discussing him. But why was Sam's sister talking to him about a *man*, if Sam had a girlfriend?

With all eyes on him, Travis had to focus. "Good news. Nothing is broken, it looks like a mild sprain. I'm going to wrap it with an Ace Bandage and give him a sling to wear for a few days, until it feels better."

"That's great news." Sam's voice oozed relief. "Thank you so much." He turned to Levi. "Did you hear that? Your arm should be feeling better in just a few days."

He bobbed his head up and down, then looked at Travis. "What are your kids?"

"Excuse me?" Travis blinked.

"Boys or girls, I mean. Why didn't you bring them to the race? Don't they like to watch you?" Levi's questions were natural and friendly, but Travis was still baffled.

Apparently they had been talking about him. He looked at Sam. "Who told you I had three kids?"

Sam waved a hand. "Let's not worry about that now. It's getting late, and we need to get him home for dinner. You said something about a sling?"

Levi kept talking. "Uncle Sammy doesn't have any kids. Mommy says that's 'cause he's gay. Gay people don't make babies."

"Levi!" Sam's face turned beet red. "It's not polite to discuss that kind of stuff with strangers."

Travis tried to keep the 'cat who ate the canary' expression on his face to a minimum. He glanced at Sam quickly then squatted in front of Levi. "It's all right, Levi. I'm not a stranger, I'm your doctor. You're absolutely right that it takes a man and a woman to make a baby. But gay people can still have children. They just have to choose other people to help them with it."

Melanie gazed at him suspiciously. "You seem to know a lot about gay people, *Dr. Travis.*"

He rose and stared back at her. "Just basic human anatomy."

Janel entered with the bandage and sling, and they proceeded to take care of the boy's arm. They'd barely finished when Melanie said, "Are we done here? I need a smoke. I'm going out to the car."

Travis tried to hide his disdain. "We're done."

"I'll walk you out," Janel led Melanie to the door.

"I'll take care of the bill and be right out," Sam advised his sister.

She nodded and left without another word to Travis.

Levi glanced up and smiled at him. "Thank you, Dr. Travis." He gave Travis' leg a quick hug, then followed his mother.

Travis stood in the doorway and blocked Sam's exit. "He's a really good kid."

"I know," Sam agreed. "You can see why this is so hard for me."

"No, I really can't. Why didn't you tell me you're gay? It's not like you didn't have a chance. You had the perfect opportunity when I told you I was."

Sam just stood there, shaking his head. "It doesn't matter. Gay or straight, I don't have time for a life right now. My sister—well, you can see how she is. She's a flipping mess, but she's all that Levi has."

"Because his father went to prison."

"Exactly. Mel's barely holding herself together, let alone taking care of a kid. I've got to be there for him. I'm taking him to school, picking him up, feeding him, making sure he bathes and does his homework and all of it. Mel works most nights, so I can't go out then. I'm living in one room of a shitty apartment. Levi has the other bedroom and Mel sleeps on the couch. Tell me when I'd have time to fit a relationship into my schedule."

Travis sighed. "That's tough, man, I agree. But a relationship doesn't have to be all about schedules. Sometimes it can be just hanging out together."

Sam blinked. "You, me and Levi? Cozy."

He shrugged. "Doesn't sound that bad to me. Listen, since I've been on call I have tomorrow off. Levi has school, right? Maybe we could get together for lunch or something."

The handsome hunk smiled at him sadly. "Lunch is probably all I have the energy for. But yeah, I could do lunch."

Travis pulled a business card from his pocket and wrote his home address and cell number on it. He handed it over with a return smile. "Shall we say about eleven?"

"Early lunch," Sam commented.

He grinned. "We're working under a time constraint. School gets out at, what? Three?"

"Yeah. Thanks, Travis. I'm looking forward to it."

"So am I." He stepped aside so Sam could leave.

"Direct me to the person I can settle up the bill with?"

"No charge today."

Sam frowned. "You can't do that."

"It's already done. Forget about it."

"We can pay our way."

"Well, if you insist, you'll have to find some other way to pay me back. Not coercing you in any way, but just saying…"

Sam paused and smiled. "Do I get to see your tattoos?"

"If you want to."

"I do. I really do."

Travis liked the hungry look in Sam's eyes. He felt the same way. "See you tomorrow, then."

Chapter Three

Friday morning, Sam showered and checked Google Maps to locate the address Travis had provided him. Unsure what to wear, he finally decided on black jeans and a white button-down shirt, left untucked. He was ready an hour before he needed to leave, but he was nervous and couldn't focus on anything but the handsome doctor and what the day might bring.

Melanie slept peacefully on the sofa as he slipped out of the door. She'd never know he was gone. He'd return with Levi at three-thirty, and all would be well. Sam headed out.

It took twenty minutes to reach the nice neighborhood Travis lived in. *Of course he lives someplace like this.* A doctor wouldn't live where he had to worry about bugs or, worse yet, rats.

Sam parked his bug in the double driveway of the large white stone house and smiled at the basketball goal above the garage doors. Levi would love a place like this. He wondered if Mel would ever be able to provide it. *Maybe if she got lucky and married a doctor who didn't mind her drug addiction.*

He shook his head to clear the negative thoughts and climbed out of his car.

The front door opened and Travis came into view. He was wearing shorts and a tank top, exposing the massive, colorful tattoos covering his skin.

Sam gave him the once-over as he climbed the front porch steps. "Holy mackerel, you weren't kidding, were you?"

The doctor grinned. "I'm told I have an obsessive personality. When I do something, I don't do it partway. It's whole hog or nothing."

"Which is not all bad." Sam paused next to him and studied the various patterns of ink on the closest arm. "Wow. You'll have to tell me the significance of all these someday."

"Someday I will. For now, come in. *Mi casa es su casa.*"

Sam stepped inside, awed at the beautiful southwest-decorated living room, which sported shades of tans, browns and blues. "Wow. This is one hell of a *casa.*"

Travis waved a hand. "It's comfortable."

Sam bit back a laugh. If the good doctor thought this place was merely 'comfortable', he wondered what he'd think about Mel's tiny infested apartment. 'Cozy' didn't even fit quite right. "Comfortable. Yeah. It's very nice, Travis."

"Are you hungry? I've prepared chicken fettuccine alfredo and a feta salad. I thought we might have a glass or two of wine, as well." He led the way into a spacious, open kitchen. Pots and pans hung from the ceiling above a center work space island. There were four seats at the kitchen bar and a table in a nook around the corner.

Sam didn't want to gush over every room though he easily could have. He sighed. "That sounds amazing.

The last pasta I ate came from a box with *Velveeta* written on the front."

"Eh, it's different when you're cooking for kids. They have peculiar appetites."

"Yeah, true, but that was what my sister was hungry for."

They laughed and Sam sat while Travis served their meal at the bar. He sat next to Sam and they talked as they ate. "I hope you don't mind, but I took the liberty of doing something for you as a surprise."

Sam savored the first bite. "Something more than this fantastic meal? I can't imagine what it could be."

Travis smiled. "I've arranged for two massage therapists to come here at one o'clock. They'll bring portable tables, and we can have dual massages for an hour this afternoon."

Sam could have fallen off his stool. "Massages? Oh my God. Have I died and gone to Heaven?"

"Oh yeah." Travis grinned over his wine glass. "You definitely have."

"You must think I'm a pathetic sad sack to pamper me this much."

The smile slipped from the doctor's face and he set his glass down. "I do *not* think that, and I'm *pampering* you because I like you, and because I can. And yeah, a part of me is doing it to get you between the sheets. Not today — don't worry about that. There's no pressure. But sometime soon, whenever you're ready, just letting you know I'll be game."

Sam gazed at him thoughtfully. "Wow. That could be the nicest thing anyone has ever said to me." He leaned in until his face was mere inches from Travis'. "Would I be too forward if I snuck a kiss right now?"

"I've been waiting for this since the first day I laid eyes on you." Travis brought their lips together in a gentle kiss.

Sam knew then he truly was in Heaven. Travis' mouth was soft and strong at the same time, the perfect combination of sweetness and heat. He opened his lips and Travis didn't waste any time allowing his tongue to dart forward. Sam met the tongue with his own, and they battled for dominance as the kiss lingered on.

He finally had to pull back to breathe.

Travis groaned. "Don't stop. Feels too good."

Sam pressed a light kiss to the corner of the doctor's mouth. "What happened to 'not today'?"

"Changed my mind. Totally changed it. I want to feel that tongue on every inch of my body. And that's just for starters."

It was Sam's turn to groan. "I want that, too. I can't wait to explore every one of those sexy tats with my mouth. But as wonderful as that sounds, you got me jazzed up for that massage and I'd hate to miss it. Or miss out on finishing this meal."

Travis pulled away. "You're right, of course. Let's eat so the food has a chance to settle. We've got time for the rest of it. We'll have another day. I'm not going anywhere, Sam."

Sam gazed at him appreciatively. "Me either." He stole one more quick kiss, then they went back to eating with big smiles on their faces.

Julie and Jill, the massage therapists, arrived shortly before one and set their tables up in the spacious living room. Following Travis' lead, Sam stripped to his boxers and climbed on one table, then covered up with the provided sheet.

The women lit candles and lowered the lights, then turned on soft music. Sam had never had a massage in a spa so he wasn't sure what to expect, but it was done very tastefully. Jill folded the sheet down to his stomach as she worked on his arms and shoulders. She then uncovered one leg at a time and massaged it. When she'd finished, he rolled onto his belly and she massaged the calf and foot of each leg before finishing with a nice, long backrub.

He didn't want to move when it was over, but the tables had to go. He carried his clothes to one bathroom and Travis took his to another. When they returned, Travis paid the women and they left, precisely an hour later.

"Wow." Sam sank into the sofa. "That was incredible. Thank you so much."

"I enjoyed it too. We'll do it again sometime." He handed Sam one of the bottles of water the women had left. "But now, I'm estimating we have about twenty minutes to neck before you have to go and pick up Levi."

Sam took a swig of water and set the bottle down. "Twenty minutes to neck? Damn, feels like high school all over again."

Travis grinned. "High school was fun. Sneaking around, furtive hand jobs in the showers, quickie blow jobs in the car…"

Sam's cock thickened. "Mmm, those things do sound like fun."

Travis straddled him and ground their groins together. "They were fun, and they will be again, when you and I have more time. I love giving head, and there won't be anything quick about it. When I devour you, I'm gonna want plenty of time."

"Aw, God." Sam panted as their mouths came together. Tongues battled again, to and fro, lingering in one mouth then the other. His cock was on fire, and he could feel Travis' was just as hard. "Use your hand now," he encouraged. "Quick can be nice, too."

"Not for our first time." Travis circled Sam's inner ear with his tongue before drawing the lobe into his mouth. "Our first time is gonna be slow and sweet, not fast, furious and sticky."

"I like sticky." Sam's voice was almost a whimper.

"And I like you—too much to do that to you."

"You're gonna make me go home and jack off, thinking of you?"

"Yep. You can picture me here, jacking off, thinking of you."

Sam groaned again as Travis sucked his neck. "Fuck, yeah."

"Oh, I like to fuck, too. Doggie style, missionary style, bent over the back of the sofa, across the kitchen table, and standing in the shower. I like to give and receive. How about you, sexy?"

"Both," Sam panted. "All of the above. At this rate I might not make it home. Forgive me if I come in my pants."

Travis laughed and pulled back. "Sorry, our twenty minutes is up. But I'll see you tonight in my dreams."

Sam wiped perspiration from his brow. "You are a horrible tease."

"And you are a good uncle who'd never be late to pick up his kid. I'll check my schedule and let you know when my next weekday off is. But maybe this weekend we could get together and do something with Levi?"

"That'd be great. Thank you."

Travis squeezed Sam's crotch as he climbed off. "No, man. Thank *you*. I'm stoked to see where this thing takes us."

"Me too. You have no idea." He rose and gathered his things.

"Text me so I'll have your number."

"Will do." He looked at Travis seriously. "Thanks again for lunch and the massage. They were both perfect."

"I thought so, too. Talk to you soon, handsome."

"You bet." Sam ogled him one more time, then mustered all the willpower he possessed to walk out.

* * * *

Travis' text notification sounded, and he reached for his phone. Nearly nine a.m., he needed to get up but was comfortable right where he was. He glanced at the screen.

The text was from his mom.

Good morning. What's on the agenda for today?

He didn't answer immediately, instead went to reread the texts he'd gotten from Sam the night before.

Lying in bed. Thinking of you makes me want to touch myself.

Wish I was there. I'd love to be the one touching you.

Text sex isn't quite as convenient as phone sex. Need two hands to type, damn it!

Call me and I'll be happy to talk dirty in your ear.

Thin walls. Sorry. Want to go to the park with Levi and me tomorrow?

What if we make it the zoo, and lunch after?

Levi would love that.

Great. Give me your address and I'll pick you up at, say, ten?

Ten is fine. We can meet you.

I'd rather we just had one car. I'll pick you up.

Okay. We'll be outside waiting for you at ten.

Sam gave an address Travis wasn't familiar with.

He'd looked it up, and realized it was a fairly shabby neighborhood. He didn't care, but felt bad for Sam and Levi. He didn't feel much for Melanie, yet. Hopefully as he got to know her he'd see whatever good qualities the rest of her family saw.

Frustration had welled in Travis. Sam was so worried about his getting too close. He was going to have to work on that.

See you in the morning, sexy thing.

Goodnight, Sam had answered.

Travis smiled at the exchange, then answered his mom.

Good morning. I'm actually going to the zoo today, then lunch with friends.

The zoo? Interesting. Have fun. Come for dinner tomorrow night? Call in the morning and let me know.

I'll call you tomorrow. Have a good day.

Travis tossed his phone on the nightstand and forced himself out of bed. A thought occurred to him and he opened the drawer of his bedside table, checking for condoms. He had half a box, and they weren't expired. That'd be enough for now, but he'd need to remember to get more. His lube supply was sufficient. He also wanted to take a new blood test, just to have it. He doubted Sam would want to see it, but he liked to be prepared.

As he climbed into the shower, he considered the ramifications of asking Sam to submit to a blood test. It seemed like a shitty thing to ask, but as a doctor he knew too well what could happen. He needed to do it, and would mention it today.

It was chilly out, so he dressed in jeans and a long-sleeved T-shirt. He always covered his tats when going out to public places. He could only imagine the looks on some parents' faces when they saw how heavily he was inked. His abilities as a doctor would immediately be called into question. Ridiculous, but that was the world he lived in.

He didn't mind covering them, in fact it made him feel like he had a sexy secret. The fact that Sam found his tats sexy was an even bigger turn on. He could not wait to get that man alone again. Next time, they wouldn't waste one moment.

Grabbing his sunglasses, Travis headed out to his Lexus. He was excited to spend time with Sam and Levi and hoped the zoo wouldn't disappoint. Some kids were into animals and some weren't. He didn't know Levi well enough to determine that, yet. But that was fixing to change.

He plugged their address into his car's GPS and headed out. Twenty minutes later he slowed to a crawl in front of a run-down-looking apartment complex, searching for addresses. He spotted Sam and Levi on the sidewalk and pulled in.

"Hey," he greeted as Sam opened the passenger front and back doors.

"Good morning." Sam shot him a look filled with promise. He held up a booster car seat. "Do you mind?"

Travis grinned at the handsome man. "Of course not." He turned to watch as Levi climbed into the back seat and his uncle fastened him in. "Hey, buddy. How are you doing today?"

"Hi, Dr. Travis! Uncle Sammy says we're going to the zoo!"

"We are. I loved the zoo when I was a kid. Do you like it?"

Levi shrugged. "I've never been."

Sam closed the back door and got into the front seat. "I can't remember the last time I've been, either."

"All right, then. This is gonna be great." Travis made sure they were both situated before taking off. "It'll take us about a half hour to get there, so everyone get comfy."

Sam glanced at him sideways. "I'm plenty comfy, right here."

Travis winked at him and glanced at the boy in his rear-view mirror. "How's the arm today, Levi?"

"It doesn't hurt when it's slinged up."

"Good." Travis grinned at Sam. "Slinged up. I like that. Might have to use it on some other patients."

Sam nodded. "I can hear you now. Okay, kid, we'll get you slinged up here in a minute."

"For sure." They made small talk on the ride and once they arrived, Travis paid the admittance fee and they entered.

Levi was immediately awestruck. He couldn't move from one exhibit to the next quickly enough. He made faces at the monkeys and strutted around like the tall giraffes. When they reached the petting zoo and he was allowed to feed the animals, he announced he never wanted to leave.

"I think the zoo was a hit." Sam leaned in to Travis with a smile on his face. "Thank you."

"You might not thank me if he pitches a fit when it's time to leave."

Sam gazed at him seriously. "Levi doesn't throw fits."

Travis grinned. "Are you kidding me? He's *six*. The occasional meltdown should be a way of life."

His handsome friend shrugged. "I can't explain it, but he's a very even-tempered kid. I don't think I've ever seen him pitch a fit or throw a tantrum of any kind."

"Wow. You're lucky. I have children in my office who melt down when we don't have the right flavor of sucker to give them when they leave."

Sam shook his head. "Not Levi."

Travis caught his eye. "Good. I'm glad. That has to make things easier for you."

"I'm fine. Don't worry about me. In fact, I was going to mention that if you don't let me pay for lunch, I don't think we can make it."

Travis could see he wasn't joking. "Lunch is no big deal."

"No? Good. Then I'll buy."

"Sam—" he started to protest.

"Look." Sam caught his hand and squeezed. "I'm not destitute. My living arrangements aren't the best right now because I choose to be there for Mel and Levi. But I have money. And I'm buying lunch today."

Travis squeezed back. "Works for me. As long as you remember that I'm here for you. If you *do* need anything, I want you to let me know."

Sam chuckled. "I'm not going to do that. We barely know each other."

Holding tight to Sam's hand, Travis nodded. "I've had that same thought recently. It's time to do something about it. I want to get to know you better." He glanced around and didn't see anyone close to them except Levi feeding some baby goats. He leaned in and planted a light kiss on Sam's mouth.

Sam smiled, surprised. "Okay, you're right. We're off to a good start this weekend."

"A very good start." Travis wanted to kiss him again, but people had wandered by and it wasn't the time. *Soon.*

Levi stood and dusted off his hands. "I'm hungry!" he announced.

Sam scratched his chin thoughtfully. "Could you go for the buffet at Mario's Pizza?"

"Yes!" Levi hopped up and down excitedly. He hugged Sam's leg then Travis'.

Travis could only watch and smile. "Looks like you said the magic words."

"Have you eaten at Mario's?"

"I don't believe so."

Levi spread his hands wide. "They have a *jillion* kinds of pizza. And if they don't have the one you want, they'll make it for you."

"True," Sam agreed. "They'll bring you a slice or the whole pie. It's decent pizza, too."

"My favorite is the macaroni and cheese pizza." Levi rubbed his stomach.

"Okay, you guys are making me hungry. Let's go!" Travis motioned for them to head out.

Levi grabbed his hand then reached for one of Sam's, and walked between them.

It felt so natural, Travis got a little choked up. He pictured himself with Sam and their own child, somewhere down the road. The idea was insane and definitely putting the cart before the horse. But it made him so damned happy, he couldn't put it out of his mind.

"What are you smiling about?" Sam whispered.

He tried to be serious. "I'm not smiling."

"Whatever. Softie."

"So sue me. I like kids."

"Hence the pediatrician gig. It's a good thing you do, or people might call you crazy."

"That's been done before. They get one look at my tattoos, and that's all it takes."

Levi glanced up. "You have chattoos? Can I see them?"

"Maybe later," Travis put him off. He wasn't sure that was a good idea. Hopefully Levi would forget. He made a mental note to be more careful and watch what he said around the boy. He wanted to spend time with Sam, and knew Levi was going to be part of the package. He'd get used to it. He was enjoying the child, but wouldn't mind some alone time with the uncle *soon*.

Sam directed him to Mario's Pizza and they went in and ate. Levi was correct, the menu seemed to have a jillion types of pizza, plus pasta, breadsticks and dessert choices. Travis didn't usually eat so many carbs but decided he didn't care. He could eat light for dinner. They talked, laughed and ate until they were all stuffed.

He sat across the booth from Sam and nudged his foot with his own.

Sam smiled, and continued the game of footsie all through lunch. He finally looked at Levi and said, "We should probably be getting home. Your mom will want to spend some time with you before she goes to work."

"Maybe she's not awake yet." Levi sounded almost hopeful.

Travis didn't want the day to end, either. "Could you text her and find out? Or would that wake her?"

Sam pulled out his phone. "No, she doesn't hear the phone when she sleeps. I'll text and see if she's up." His fingers flew over the keyboard.

They drank another round of beverages and Sam glanced at his phone. "She's not up. I'll just text her to give me a shout when she wants us to come home."

"Good." Levi grinned.

Travis felt the same way. "Do you guys like video games?"

"Yes!" the boy shouted. "We had a PlayStation but my dad had to sell it."

Nice. Travis bit back his first thought and instead offered, "I have one, and I have some pretty good games for it. Would you like to come over and check it out?"

"Can we?" Levi's eyes lit up like a Christmas tree.

Sam glanced at his watch. "Sure, I guess. Just remember, when your mom texts, we'll have to leave."

"Okay." He jumped up.

"Let's go wash you up, Mr. Pizza sauce face." Sam looked at Travis. "We'll be back."

"I'll be right here." He watched them go fondly. He was falling hard, but he wasn't sure if it was for Sam or the image of the family he was building in his mind. Either way, it was a good feeling, and a sense of satisfaction settled in the pit of his stomach. "Sleep well, Melanie," he whispered to himself.

They returned and he ushered them out to his car, then to his house. Levi moved through the rooms with another look of awe on his face.

"Big place, huh?" Sam dropped onto the sofa.

"Yeah." The boy's voice was breathy. "Really big." He looked at Travis. "You live here all by yourself?"

He suddenly felt guilty, and wished he had an answer that sounded more noble than a simple 'yes'. "I do." He changed the subject quickly. "How about that PlayStation?"

Travis pulled out the system and three controllers, then let Levi choose from his games. They started playing and were having so much fun, Travis lost track of time.

It was only when Levi mentioned, "I'm thirsty," that he glanced at his watch.

"Holy cow, it's almost dinner time. Levi, I've got milk or water, what would you like?"

"Milk, please."

He stood to get it. "Sam?"

Sam grinned sheepishly. "Do you have anything with some fizz to it?"

"No soda in this house. I've got beer, though."

Sam seemed to consider it.

"You're not driving. Want one?"

"Sure."

Travis brought a beer, water for himself, and a glass of milk for Levi to the living room.

Sam was texting again. "Mel still hasn't answered."

"Must have been tired," Travis commented.

"Yeah." Sam looked worried.

"So." Travis hoped to cheer him up. "I've got some chicken I could toss on the grill if you two would like to stay for dinner. We could grill some vegetables, maybe add a salad."

"Please, please, please." Levi was hopping up and down again, swinging Sam's hand.

Sam winced. "If your mom calls, we'll have to leave. I'd hate for Dr. Travis to go to all that work if we need to go."

Travis shrugged. "What if we invite her?"

Sam blinked. "Invite her? Here?"

"Sure. She could come eat with us before she goes to work."

"That'd be great," Levi decided for them.

Sam could only nod.

"Come on, then. I'll need some help to put this feast together."

They prepped the food and carried the plate of chicken to the back patio.

Levi placed the utensils he was holding on the patio table, then ran around the large fenced yard. "Do you have a dog?" he asked hopefully.

"No, sorry." Travis lit the grill.

"Plenty of room for one," Levi added.

Travis laughed. "True enough. I'll give it some thought."

Sam rolled his eyes. "You don't have to agree with everything he says, you know. You can tell him, 'No, I don't have a dog because they require lots of work and they crap all over the back yard.'"

Travis grinned. "That's not why I don't have one."

"Why, then?" Sam sat in a patio chair next to him.

"I don't know. Because I never thought of it, I guess. I like dogs."

"For Christ's sake, don't get one on our account." His cell phone rang and Sam answered it. "Hello. Hey, Mel."

Travis couldn't hear what she was saying, but he definitely heard her yelling.

"Calm down," Sam muttered. "We're with Travis, and we're fixing dinner. He said you're welcome to join us before work if you like."

The offer was met with more shouting.

"Mel, take it easy. I texted you earlier and you never answered me. I would have brought him home sooner if you had."

Travis heard a string of swear words.

"Fine, I'll bring him home now. You'll still have a couple hours with Levi." Sam appeared surprised. "You what? Well, if you're meeting someone for dinner, why would I go to the trouble of bringing him home right now? It's a twenty minute trip. You'll just have a few minutes to see him."

More shouting. Travis' love for Melanie was *not* growing.

Sam set his jaw. "No, Mel, I won't. We're not interrupting what we're doing so I can bring him home and you can see him for five minutes. He's having fun. If you can calm down, I'll put him on the phone and you can say goodnight."

Travis couldn't believe he heard more swearing.

Sam face's contorted into a frown. He checked to be sure Levi was out of earshot. "What-the-fuck-ever, Mel. I won't put him on with you in this condition. Tomorrow's Sunday, you can spend the day with him if you bother to get yourself up and out of bed. Yeah, that's right. Goodnight." Sam ended the call.

He looked shaken, and Travis felt awful. "I'm sorry if I caused this."

"You didn't. She's high again, and never reasonable in this condition."

Travis frowned. "And she's getting ready to drive to work?"

"No, a friend is picking her up. They're going to dinner before work. She doesn't drive under the influence."

Travis plunked the chicken on the grill harder than he needed to. "No, she just works under the influence."

"She's a waitress. It's not rocket science."

"I'm surprised her boss puts up with it."

Sam stood. "I can't say for sure, but I think he's the one who scores the stuff, and they do it together. Among other things."

"Ah. A boss with benefits."

"Right. I'm going to snag one more beer. You sure you don't want one?"

Travis thought about it. They had an hour until dinner, and hopefully Sam and Levi would stick around for a while after. One beer now wouldn't hurt. "Sure. Thanks."

Sam shot him a wink before heading inside.

Travis' heart soared.

Chapter Four

Sam entered the kitchen, closing the door behind him. He leaned against a bar stool, taking a moment to collect himself. Mel had been worse than usual tonight. He couldn't tell if she was jealous that he'd made a new friend who Levi liked, or if it was something more.

Her boss was a real sleazeball. The guy had been friends with Rob, Mel's ex, but had somehow escaped the drug sting that had brought Rob down. He hadn't learned from it, though. Judging by Mel's behavior, they were as deep into the shit as ever. Sam couldn't shake the feeling that his sister was floundering, and there was nothing he could do about it.

Travis stuck his head in the door. "You okay?"

Sam wiped his eyes quickly. "Yeah. Just snooping in your cupboards."

"Right." The doctor chuckled.

Levi squeezed past Travis in the doorway. "Gotta pee." He headed down the hall. "I know. Wash my hands."

"Thank you," Sam called after him. He glanced at Travis. "He's making himself right at home."

Travis stepped in. "Good." He reached for Sam's hips and drew him close, then wiped Sam's cheeks with his thumbs. "I want you both to feel at home. And I don't want you to feel like you need to hide your emotions from me."

Sam grabbed Travis' face and kissed him firmly on the mouth.

Travis responded, pressing their hips together and bucking.

The solid erection Sam felt matched his own, and was more tantalizing than anything he'd ever recalled in his life. He wanted Travis in every way possible. Somehow, they'd need to find a way to make it work. "Want you," he murmured through salty kisses.

"*Need* you," Travis responded. "And soon."

Sam heard the toilet flush and water running in the distance. He kissed Travis one more time then pulled away. "Maybe tomorrow, if Mel is doing okay, and wants to spend some time with Levi."

"Tomorrow would be great. Whenever you can get away. Shoot me a text to make sure I'm home. I usually go for a ride on Sunday mornings, but after that I'll be free all day."

"Will you be up for a different kind of ride Sunday afternoon?" Sam teased.

Travis' eyes twinkled. "You know I will."

"We might only have a couple of hours."

"You'd be amazed at what I can do in a couple of hours."

Sam groaned, willing away the hard-on in his jeans.

Levi re-entered the kitchen and headed straight for the back door. "There's a lot of smoke," he commented.

Travis glanced out of the patio door. "Shoot. I better get back out there."

"You burning our dinner?" Sam joked.

"Something's burning, that's for sure." Travis grinned and slipped outside with Levi.

"I'll be right out. Grabbing those beers." Sam did, and joined them out back.

They played tag and other games with Levi in between cooking duties, and when the food was ready they ate on the patio. Sam had never felt so comfortable with a man he barely knew before. He shook his head to clear out that thought which kept plaguing him. He was starting to know Travis quite well, and so far he liked what he'd learned. The doctor was intelligent about many different subjects and seemed capable and willing to do many things. Sam's mind wandered to the bedroom and a thrill zipped down his spine. He could only imagine how capable Travis was in that department. He couldn't wait to find out.

His comfort came too easy and caused a nervous niggling in the pit of his stomach. He was becoming attached too soon, and worried that Levi was, too. The three of them could play house all day but it didn't change their reality. And when it ended, he and Levi would be the odd men out. Sam needed to protect his heart, and more importantly, he needed to protect Levi.

"Can we play more video games?" the boy asked as they cleaned up after dinner.

"I don't think so," Sam answered quickly. "We probably need to go."

"Do you have to?" Travis' eyes beckoned him. "Can't you stick around a while longer? Mel's at work, right? We could watch a movie."

"Movie!" Levi repeated with excitement evident.

Sam smiled at his nephew then looked at Travis. "He'll fall asleep as soon as he slows his roll."

"I won't!" Levi insisted.

Sam knew better. It had been a full day.

"So?" Travis shrugged. "Let him. We can carry him to the car later." His expression changed to one of pleading.

Unable to resist, Sam gave in. "Why not?"

Levi plopped down in the middle of the sofa but Travis seemed to have other ideas.

"Look, Levi." The seat at the end of the sectional was a recliner with a foot rest that extended out. "This is my special comfy seat. Would you like to sit here?"

"Yes!" He scooted down, leaving the rest of the sofa free.

Sam grinned. Without the boy sitting between them, their movie-watching experience was about to get a lot more interesting.

Travis let Levi choose from his DVD collection and the boy chose *Home Alone*.

"Seriously?" Sam teased as Travis sat next to him.

"It's a classic." Travis nodded emphatically. He reached for Sam's hand and held it.

Ten minutes into the movie, before the star of the show even got left home alone, Levi was out. He curled up in the recliner with his back to them.

Travis stood and pulled a soft fleece throw from the front closet. He covered Levi gently, then returned to his spot on the sofa. "Now. Where were we?"

Sam shook his head sadly. "You know we can't."

"I know. But a few kisses won't hurt a thing."

Grinning, Sam reached for the sexy hunk. "True." They embraced and kissed when their lips met. Gentle to begin with, the kiss grew more fervent the longer it went on. Sam opened his mouth fully and groaned when Travis' tongue made itself right at home. Travis caressed wherever he could reach. It all felt so good. *So right.*

His cock throbbed within the confines of his jeans. When Travis panted for breath he took advantage of the break and whispered, "You were wrong. Part of me does hurt." He bucked his hips.

Travis rubbed a hand over Sam's crotch, groping through the denim. "Sorry, baby. Wish there was more that I could do."

"Soon," Sam reminded.

Travis nodded. "Very soon." He moved his mouth to Sam's ear so he could whisper in it. "I'm gonna lick your big, fat cock from base to tip and back again... Over and over. Your balls are gonna draw up so tight. I'll wedge a finger into your sweet, tight ass and work your prostate until you can't stand any more. Then I'll just smile and swallow when you shoot your hot, creamy load down my throat."

"Aw, God." Sam wanted that more than anything.

Travis sucked his earlobe and continued. "Once you're good and satisfied, I'm gonna lube up my hand and see how many fingers I can stick inside your hot bod. Can you take three? Will you beg for four?"

Sam could only whimper.

"Maybe I'll stick my tongue in there and give you a nice rim job. It probably won't last long, though. My cock will be so hard it'll be ready to burst. I'll be desperate to get inside you. I'll roll on a rubber raincoat and grease myself up so I can plunge balls deep into your burning hot ass."

"Aw, fuck." Sam was nearly delirious.

"That's right, I'm gonna fuck you so hard, you'll think about it for days after. I'll pound my cock in and out of your hole until you're begging for mercy. You'll come again with very little stimulation. While I'm emptying my seed into your aching ass, you'll blow all over yourself. Once I can think straight again, I'll lick you clean and kiss you so you can taste your own cum. I'll keep kissing and licking and sucking until we're both so hot we're ready to go again."

Sam turned his face to meet Travis' mouth. "I'm ready to go right now. Your sexy play-by-play has me turned on."

"Good." Travis rubbed Sam's crotch again. "Think about me tonight when you're lying in bed. I'll be thinking about you when I'm jerking off."

Leaning in for another kiss, Sam added, "Don't worry. You're all I seem to think about these days."

"Glad to hear it." Travis glanced over at Levi, who was still sleeping with his back to them. He dove back into a kiss, which Sam never wanted to end.

The movie did end, and they came up for air. Sam's face felt raw and tender from an hour of close contact with Travis' three-day beard growth.

Travis pressed a hand to his cheek. "You're red. I'm sorry. I should have shaved."

"Don't shave." Sam shook his head. "I love the way you look with scruff, and I love kissing you. I have no complaints." He glanced around. "Other than the fact that we have to leave and unfortunately, you have to take us."

Travis leaned back against the sofa and eyed him thoughtfully. "You could always stay."

"If it was just me I'd take you up on that offer in a heartbeat. But I can't do that to Levi."

"Levi slept through *Home Alone* and our incredibly hot make-out session. If we tucked him into my spare room he'd probably sleep through the night."

Sam nodded. "He probably would, and then he'd wake up in an unfamiliar place. Then he'd come looking and find me in your bed. He might be frightened, and I know for a fact his mom would be furious. I can't, Travis."

"I know. But I had to ask, all the same."

"Understood. I'm sorry you have to get out. I could call a cab."

"Oh hell no. I picked you up and I'm taking you home. Besides, it means we'll get to spend another half hour together. I enjoy being with you, Sam. I'll take every minute I can get." He batted his eyelashes.

Sam sighed. "You're amazing."

Travis grinned. "See how well you know me already!"

They laughed and stood to get ready to go. Sam carried his sleeping nephew to the back seat of the car and belted him in to keep him upright.

Travis drove them home with one hand on the wheel and the other holding on to one of Sam's. They talked quietly and when he pulled up in front of the apartment complex, he shut the car off.

"You don't have to get out," Sam said. "I've got him."

"I'll go with and unlock the door."

"That's not necessary." Sam didn't want him seeing their living quarters.

"Sam." Travis squeezed his hand. "You don't have to worry about what I'll think. I don't care about your sister's apartment. I just want to give you a hand."

Sam gazed into his eyes. "How can you know what I'm thinking?"

"Because I can see right through those clear blue eyes and into your soul. You're a good person, but you worry too much. I care for you, Sam, and I care about you. I want to be part of your life. That includes seeing where you sleep at night."

"It's embarrassing," Sam admitted.

"It shouldn't be." Travis leaned in and whispered, "I'm the guy who plans to eat your ass, remember? Nothing should be embarrassing between us. Which reminds me, my blood has always tested negative and I have results from a couple of months ago. I haven't been with anyone since. I'll take a new test, though, just to be safe."

Sam smiled. "Great minds think alike. I had blood drawn a few days ago and the results were negative." He reached for his wallet.

Travis stopped him. "I trust you."

"I trust you, too." Sam gazed into his eyes. "But I do have to be careful. You'd be awfully easy to fall for, Dr. Travis Nelson."

Travis' smile was endearing. "Go right ahead and fall, handsome. I'll be here to catch you, any time and every time."

Sam cupped Travis' face as they kissed, hungry again for the taste of him. As their tongues battled, his mind wandered.

He prayed for the same things each night. For Mel to be healed physically and mentally and become a happy person and the mother she was meant to be. For Levi to grow up happy, healthy and secure, and always feeling safe, full, protected and very much loved.

Tonight Sam's prayers would be different. Tonight he was going to pray with all his heart that Mel would be up to keeping Levi for a few hours the next day, so he could spend some time in the loving embrace of Dr. Travis Nelson. He couldn't think of anything he wanted more.

* * * *

Travis rode his bike fifteen miles Sunday morning then showered and called his parents, all before ten a.m. He knew Melanie would probably sleep until noon so if Sam was going to have any free time it'd be afternoon to evening. He didn't know if she worked Sundays. Maybe they'd have more time if she didn't.

He did some laundry, put fresh sheets on the bed, and vacuumed and dusted his already fairly clean house. Nervous energy raced through him, and he couldn't just sit. Somewhere around twelve-thirty he had a sinking feeling— *What if Sam can't get away?* Their whole day depended on his deadbeat sister and whether or not she felt like spending time with her son.

As he paced, he forced himself to temper his thoughts. Melanie was Sam's twin sister. He loved her deeply, or he wouldn't be doing what he was for her and her boy. If Travis wanted to be part of Sam's life, he'd have to tread gently where the sister was concerned. Calling her a deadbeat wouldn't win him any points, even if that was how she came across to him.

His phone vibrated and Travis glanced at the screen.

Want some company?

Sam had added a devil emoticon. He smiled and typed back.

Is that a hypothetical question? One that really doesn't require an answer?

I know what hypothetical means.

Travis felt like an idiot.

Sorry. Get your ass over here.

On my way.

He pocketed his phone, his heart racing. *Finally.* Time alone with Sam. His dream lover for the past week would finally be here in real life, and they'd be alone. It was almost too good to be true.

When his bell rang half an hour later, Travis tried not to rip the door off its hinges. He opened it carefully, as if he actually contained any self-control at that point. "Hey," he said nonchalantly.

"Hey." Sam stepped inside and closed the door behind him. When he turned to face Travis again, they both had the same expressions on their faces.

Travis pulled him into his arms and pressed their lips together.

Sam opened his mouth and they kissed hungrily, tongues probing, hands exploring.

"Finally," Travis sighed after catching a breath.

"Feels like we've been waiting for this forever," Sam agreed. He unbuttoned the collar of Travis' shirt. "Don't want to wait any longer."

"No reason to wait." Travis reached for the hem of Sam's T-shirt and pulled it over the sexy hunk's head. The chest he exposed was nearly hairless, save for a few wiry tufts on the sculpted pecs. A fine trail of light brown hair extended south from his belly button, into faded denims. Travis' mouth watered. He unsnapped the jeans and shoved the waistband down.

He uncovered a pair of light blue boxers and lowered them along with the denims, allowing Sam's cock to spring free. The specimen unfolded and lengthened once it was no longer confined, and Travis held his breath. Long and deliciously thick, Sam's shaft was as impressive as any he'd ever seen. "Aw, Jesus," he muttered, staring. "I'm one lucky son of a bitch."

Sam chuckled and kicked out of his shoes and pants. He reached down and tossed his socks aside. "Oh really? And here I was thinking *I'm* the lucky one." With the last of Travis' buttons undone, he shoved the shirt off until it dropped to the floor. Sam unfastened Travis' jeans and both of them together shoved them down, exposing his unmarked cock.

Travis held his breath while Sam checked him out. His own cock had risen to the occasion as soon as it was freed, and was now bobbing between them.

"Oh God," Sam murmured. "Your tats are the sexiest thing ever. Then when I see the flesh that's *not* inked…" He glanced behind Travis and checked out his ass. "I didn't think you could get any hotter. Jesus, Trav, I just want to eat you up. Shall we move to the bedroom, because I'm fixing to get started here in about thirty seconds." He glanced at Travis and licked his lips.

Travis smiled. "Do we really have to wait that long?" He reached for Sam's cock and led his new lover down the hall. "Right this way, stud. I think a double sixty-nine would be the perfect way to get the ball rolling, so to speak. I want to eat you up, too."

Tossing back the covers on his king-sized bed, Travis climbed in and patted the spot next to him.

Sam joined him on the bed, and they kissed and caressed backs and shoulders again.

"Just so you know," Travis murmured, "Lube and condoms are in the drawer to the left of the bed. Help yourself, as desired."

"I will," Sam panted and dove back into a kiss. "I've been dreaming about this moment, trying to decide where to start. So many possibilities."

"Anything goes, man." Travis reached for Sam's balls and tugged gently. "I want to experience everything with you."

"Me too. And I want to explore every inch of this ink. I'm going to lick it, suck it and come all over it. I'm gonna make *you* come all over it, so I can rub it in. Of course that'll make me want to lick it and suck it again."

"A vicious cycle," Travis agreed. He pressed Sam's head to his shoulder, ready for the licking and sucking to begin. "Start now," he encouraged.

With a throaty growl, Sam nipped the flesh before he began the promised torture. His mouth felt warm and inviting, his strokes alternating between gentle and something more intense. By the time he'd gotten his mouth to Travis' groin, Travis was nearly ready to burst.

"Aw, God." He bucked his hips, desiring direct contact on his aching shaft.

"I haven't made it down each leg yet. I see a tiger down there that really caught my eye."

Travis groaned. "You'll find two tigers, a panther and some other animals down there. But if you think I can hold off while you inflict that sensuous torment down my legs, you're sadly mistaken, buddy. I'll come all over myself without much more provocation needed."

"Mmm." Sam started down one inked thigh. "I'd like to see that." He changed directions and settled in front of Travis' cock. "Later. Right now, my mouth is going to be the one that brings this bad boy home for the first time."

"Yeah, do it," Travis grunted. "Straddle me and fuck my face while you're at it. Fill my mouth with your juicy, thick cock."

"My kind of man." Sam chuckled and did as requested.

Travis opened wide when the bulky shaft was lowered on top of him. The first taste was salty and musky and nearly made him come on the spot. He tried to maintain his composure so he didn't shoot prematurely, but it was going to be tough. Sam tasted so good, and it felt amazing to have him fucking his mouth at the same time that he sucked Travis' cock. "Mmm," he encouraged, devouring the shaft and bucking his hips.

Sam paused and pulled back. "Too much?"

"Uh-uh," Travis replied, not wanting to release the savory shaft. It had settled nicely down his throat and he wasn't gagging, so he didn't want to move. "Moh." His muffled plea was nearly unintelligible, but he wanted to proceed. He was oh so ready for more.

"More, eh?" Sam chuckled. "You got it, man. Take my length down your throat, suck it good. I'm just going to nibble your tasty cockhead for a few minutes. It's the prettiest shade of purple, and the slit is oozing pre-cum. You're close, I can tell." He stroked the shaft firmly. "I want you to come, Travis. Shoot your wad into my mouth so I can taste your heat. I'm gonna let some of it dribble out and rub it on your ink, so I can enjoy it twice."

Travis was in heaven, his mouth stuffed with his man and his orgasm so close he could already feel it. Sam's sexy talk sent him over the edge and he shattered, bright white lights claiming his vision as shudders of ecstasy ripped through the rest of him. He convulsed again and again, savoring Sam's warm mouth as his lover coaxed out his seed.

Sam switched to using his hand, allowing the last few pulses of cum to coat Travis' thighs. He continued to jerk Travis' cock and allowed his mouth to follow the sticky streams. His licking and sucking sent shivers and chills directly to Travis' core.

The climax had been as perfect as he could have hoped for. His recent hand jobs, even with Sam's image to jack himself to, had been mostly unfulfilling and unsatisfying. This right here... This was the real thing.

He grasped each of Sam's thighs and squeezed them tightly as he worked the shaft deeper down his throat.

"Oh, yeah," Sam muttered as he cleaned the sticky seed from Travis' flesh. "Your mouth feels like a vise, holding me so tight. I'm close, baby. I'm gonna blow right down your throat."

"Mmm-hmm," Travis encouraged and squeezed the firm thighs harder. Snaking one hand behind, he pried open the clenched butt cheeks and pressed one finger to Sam's tight, puckering hole.

"Jesus!" A shudder went through Sam's body. "You really know how to treat a guy. Here." He leaned up and grabbed Travis' hand, inserting the index finger into his mouth. Sam got it good and wet, then returned to position and arched his back. "Now fuck me with that finger, and see how fast you can make me come."

A thrill raced down Travis' spine. He pried the ass cheeks apart again and this time worked the wet finger into the tight hole. His inner groan was echoed by a loud, desirous groan from his lover.

"Yeah, man. Fuck my ass with that finger. Stick it in me hard and fast."

Travis did, and felt Sam's balls immediately respond. Climax was imminent, and Travis had no doubts it was going to be good for both of them.

"Aw, fuck!" Sam shouted. "I'm coming!" His body tensed and muscles tightened as he shattered.

Hot, ropy cum shot down Travis' throat and he forced himself to relax and not gag. After a few pulses he pushed away, leaving only the cockhead in his mouth. He wanted to taste the offering, wanted it to fill his mouth and overflow. There was plenty of creamy cum to accommodate. Travis eased his finger out of the pulsing ass and returned his grip to a hand on each thigh, holding tight until Sam stopped shooting and his body ceased quivering.

"Oh my fucking God." Sam rose and turned around, coming to rest with his head on Travis' shoulder and one arm and leg thrown possessively across his body. "That was fucking incredible."

Travis ran his fingers over Sam's sweat-slicked back. "You talk naughty during sex."

Sam smiled at him sheepishly. "Sorry. I get carried away."

"I *like* it. No one ever talks naughty around me, in my line of work. For some reason, it really pushed me over the edge."

"*You* pushed me over the edge. That was as amazing as I knew it would be. Thank you, Trav. Thank you so much."

Travis wrapped his arms around Sam. "Don't thank me yet. I'm not anywhere near finished with you." A horrible thought occurred and he had to ask, "You don't have to go, do you?"

"No, not yet. Mel doesn't have to work today, and she was taking Levi to the park with a friend who also has a son. I think Pete's four. He's a cute kid."

"A responsible friend, I hope?" Travis couldn't imagine two stoned women putting two little boys in a car, but stupider things had been known to happen.

"Oh yeah, Ronna's all right. She's a straight arrow, far as I can tell. Her husband's in the military, deployed overseas right now."

Travis didn't mention what he was thinking. *That doesn't mean the wife is a straight arrow.* He didn't want to talk about Melanie and her friends. His cock was pulsing again, and he had better things to do. "Good." He changed the subject. "So where were we?"

"You were saying how you aren't finished yet."

Pressing Sam's shoulders to the mattress, Travis rose above him and reached for the lube and a foil packet. "Oh, that's right. I think I was getting ready to eat your ass. Before I slide inside and fuck you senseless."

Sam closed his eyes and smiled. "That won't take much. I'm already feeling a bit groggy. And deliriously happy."

Travis pressed Sam's legs open and settled between them. He examined the thin trail of hair leading from the belly button to the thicker thatch surrounding the gorgeous fleshy cock. "Mmm, me too. Damn, you're fine. I could suck that dick again if I didn't have something a little different in mind."

"I'm at your disposal." Sam ran one hand through Travis' hair. "You do whatever you want to do. I'm content to go along for the ride."

Travis buried his nose in the crack of Sam's ass. "I'm going to ride you, so hard. I'll be on you like a cowboy on a bucking bronco." He lapped the crack with his tongue a few times before nudging it into Sam's hole. "Mmm."

"Oh yeah." Sam thrashed beneath him. "Eat that ass. Get it good and ready to fuck."

He submerged his tongue as deeply as he could get it and wiggled it around. The tight outer ring felt amazing, and for the first time Travis found himself wishing he had a longer tongue. He played there for several more minutes and could sense when his lover needed more. *I'm ready, too.*

The tight muscles gripped and made pulling his tongue out tricky. When Travis was free he sat up, chuckling. "Damn, baby. Your ass didn't want to let me go."

Sam gazed at him affectionately. "That was all me, man. I'd be happy if you stayed there forever."

Travis rolled a rubber over his shaft and greased it. "Oh, but this will make you happy, too. Eight inches, deep inside your tiny channel. I'm gonna fill you up, stud." He inserted one slick finger to test Sam's readiness, working it side to side.

"Do it," Sam encouraged. "I want that beast inside me. *Now*."

"Anything you want, you got it." Travis removed his hand and pressed the tip of his cock to the entrance. "I'm gonna own this ass before long." He drove in, pausing halfway to allow Sam a moment to acclimate.

His lover nodded and Travis dove in the rest of the way. When his balls hit flesh, he stopped to enjoy the sensations. Sam looked so gorgeous beneath him, he leaned down and pressed a light kiss to his lips.

With a growl, Sam wrapped his hands around Travis' neck and shoulders and brought him closer to deepen the kiss. They rocked together, kissing and fucking, until Travis could barely breathe. He leaned up and grabbed the headboard for purchase, then gritted his teeth and fucked with all the intensity he could muster.

As an orgasm churned in his balls, he reached down and clasped Sam's leaking shaft. A few good pumps and they were both coming, shouting, and eventually laughing and rolling together on the bed.

Sam held him tight and gazed into his eyes. "You already do, baby."

"Hmm?" Travis was barely coherent anyway, he figured he must have blacked out and missed something.

Sam smiled. "You already own my ass. From this day forward, nobody touches it but you."

Travis nearly came again. He reached for the beautiful face in front of him and began kissing everywhere he could reach. "It's a deal," he finally murmured. "Same goes, by the way."

Sam waggled his eyebrows. "Good. Now lie back. I'm headed down to check out my real estate."

Chapter Five

Sam closed his laptop computer and pushed away from his desk. He'd gotten his work caught up, his latest articles had all been accepted and he'd been paid for them. It had taken the better part of a month, but he'd finally found a manageable routine juggling his job, Mel, Levi and Travis.

Travis. Just thinking about him caused Sam's cock to thicken and created a dopey smile which stayed on his face more and more these days. They stole hours together whenever they could manage it. The doctor had one day off each week, not counting most weekends, and with Levi in school they made the best of that time. They spent roughly six of those seven hours in bed, or as Travis had promised, bent over the sofa, fucking on the kitchen table, or pressed up against the steamy tiles as they fucked in the shower. They did it in every room, in every position imaginable, and as many times as one of them could manage it.

On Travis' work days, Sam was waiting for him when he got home and they'd enjoy a couple of intimate hours before Sam had to head back to watch Levi. On

Saturdays they'd take his nephew to the park or the zoo, and they'd even made a few Cubbies baseball games. They'd fix dinner together and enjoy family activities, which Levi seemed to love.

Mel was even doing better, and often spent Sundays with Levi and their friends Ronna and Pete. Depending if Travis was on call or not, Sam would either use that time to get some work done, or help Travis with housework or other chores he'd ignored all week. They usually lasted about an hour before they wound up in bed again. The laundry always got washed and dried, but not always folded or put away. Sam didn't care, and knew that his lover didn't either.

Lover. Partner. Trav called him by both titles and Sam couldn't have been happier. They hadn't actually discussed their relationship but things were good, Sam had no doubts about that.

Glancing at his watch, he saw it was nearly time to pick Levi up from school. He strolled out to the living room and saw Mel sitting on the sofa, texting someone. "Hey," he said.

She glanced up and smiled. "Hey." She kept texting.

"It's almost time to get Levi. Are you able to go for him today?"

Mel stood and tucked her phone into her jeans pocket. "Can we both go? I was hoping to talk to you."

The hair on the back of Sam's neck prickled. "O-kay. What's up?"

She grabbed his arm. "Come on. We'll talk on the way. Can you drive? I'd have to stop and get gas if we took my car."

He felt in his pocket for his keys, and nodded. As they walked out to his car he couldn't resist adding, "Mel, you know you need to keep better track of these things.

I won't always be here to fetch him, and his teacher really hates it when you're late getting him."

They got into the Volkswagen and buckled up before Sam drove.

She tossed her hair over one shoulder. "His teacher is queer and he just plain hates *me*. I think he prefers you to pick Levi up, for obvious reasons."

Sam shook his head. "Please don't call people queer. The way you say it sounds like a bad thing."

Mel looked out of the passenger window. "I almost called him a fag, but I knew you'd get pissed at that. Guess I was right."

He scoffed. "Um, you think? Geez, Mel. You can be a bitch sometimes but I don't call you that."

His sister laughed. "Why not? Derek does. I don't care."

"Derek." Sam snorted. *Her boss is such a class act.*

"Yeah, that's what I wanted to talk to you about. Derek needs a place to stay for a while. I told him he could crash with us."

Sam was stunned and tried to process that bit of news. "When's he moving in?"

"Maybe tonight. He'll probably give me a ride to work then we'll both come back together."

"Tonight? That doesn't give me any time to find another place, Mel."

"Oh, I don't expect you to find another place. I still need you to watch Levi. I was just thinking, we might have to switch bedrooms. Derek sleeps nude, and Levi doesn't need to see that. You either, for that matter. You might try to steal him." She laughed.

Sam was trying to wrap his mind around her rambling and ignored the jab. "So you want to switch with me, and I'll sleep on the sofa?"

"It seems like the best solution. I mean, we'll need some privacy anyway. I guess we could have Levi sleep on the couch. I'm just afraid Derek might wake him when we come in at night."

"Levi needs his bedroom," Sam said firmly. *So do I.* "This is really selfish of you, Mel. I'm only staying there to give you a hand with him. We agreed from the beginning that I needed my own space since I work from home."

She shrugged. "You can still use the bedroom for that. Hell, you can sleep in the bed until we get there. We'd just have to wake you up then."

Share bed sheets with Mel and Derek? Sam shivered at the thought. "I don't think so, sis. It sounds to me like you need to hire a sitter to watch Levi. She can leave when you get home."

Mel sighed loudly. "Now who's being selfish? I told you, I still need you to watch him. But I promised Derek a place to stay, so we have to find a way to make this work."

Sam couldn't believe what she was telling him. "So basically, you're just using me, is that right? For whatever you need, and whenever you need it. I think I've been pretty reasonable about things up to now, Mel."

"*You're* being reasonable? You're getting a free place to live out of this deal, so don't act like you're such a martyr."

His jaw could have hit the road passing under their wheels. "Only because you said I didn't have to pay rent! I spring for all the utilities, which in that un-insulated rat trap is almost as much as rent. I'm also buying food and necessities for the three of us."

"Levi and I hardly eat anything. Stop being so dramatic!"

Sam was livid. He raised a palm to face her. "No, you stop. This is bullshit. If you bring Derek home to live, then Derek can babysit for you and pay your bills. I'm leaving."

"You little shit!" Mel struck out at him, slapping his hand and shoving it down.

"Quit it!" he demanded, more bothered by what he'd just said than by her striking out at him. *I can't trust Levi's care to Derek. I can barely entrust him to Mel.* He shook his head. "No, that was a stupid fucking thing to say. I won't go without Levi. You can't take care of him, and neither can that stoner boss of yours. Levi and I will find somewhere else to go."

She snorted with disbelief. "You're joking, right? Like you're gonna take my kid."

He shook his head. "You can still see him after school until you go to work, but we just won't be living there. Maybe he can stay over with you nights you don't have to go in, if you think you can keep yourself clean for that long."

Mel's face twisted into something furious and ugly. She smacked his shoulder and pounded his arm. "You are a stupid, ungrateful shit! I can't believe after everything I've done for you—"

Sam fended her off. "Stop it! You're going to make me wreck. After everything *you* have done for *me*? Are you fucking out of your mind?"

She grabbed for the steering wheel. "So wreck! Who cares!" She pointed the car into oncoming traffic.

He panicked and forced the wheel in the opposite direction, overcompensating. The Bug went up on two wheels and teetered there for a moment.

"Stop it, you stupid fucker!" Mel screeched. She leaned toward him.

Sam felt the car topple. "Hang on!" he yelled, and braced himself.

* * * *

Travis had just finished with his last patient on Friday afternoon when his cell phone rang. He pulled it from his pocket and saw Sam's number. Smiling, he stepping into his office. "Hey there," he said with sultry inflections.

"Trav, I need your help." Sam sounded out of breath and unnatural.

His heart skipped a beat. "What is it?"

"Mel and I were just in an accident. I'm okay, but my car is toast. I'm not sure about her. I mean, she's alive, but unconscious. The ambulance just took her to Cook County General. Another one is going to take me."

"God, Sam!" He forced himself to remain calm. "If you're okay, why the ambulance?"

"I might have a broken wrist or something. I have to go now. But I need someone to pick up Levi from school. I hate to ask, but there's no one else."

"I can go. Jefferson Elementary, right?"

"Yes. His teacher is Mr. Crawford. I'll call him real quick and give him your name. You'll probably have to show ID."

"Well, I would hope so. I'm leaving now, Sam. I'll bring him to Cook County as soon as I can."

"Thank you, Trav. See you soon." Sounding relieved, he ended the call.

Travis gathered his things quickly and told his nurse he was leaving. Driving as fast as the speed limit allowed, he made it to the school in decent time. He entered the front office and told the woman behind the counter, "I'm supposed to pick up Levi Madison. Levi's uncle called his teacher, Mr. Crawford."

She nodded. "One moment." The woman went to an adjoining room and returned with a sandy-haired man who had Levi by the hand.

"Dr. Trav!" Levi shot out and hugged his leg.

Travis smiled. Sam's nephew had picked up on the nickname, and used it often. Travis liked hearing it from both of them. He patted Levi's back. "Hey, buddy. Sorry to be late." He glanced at the teacher. "Mr. Crawford? I'm Dr. Travis Nelson."

"Colton Crawford." He extended a hand and they shook. "I hope you understand that I have to ask for ID."

"Of course." Travis showed him his driver's license. "I'm Levi's pediatrician and a friend of the family."

"Thank you." Mr. Crawford turned to Levi. "Levi, we forgot your backpack in the classroom. Would you go get it please? We'll wait right here."

"I'll go with you," the school secretary offered. She took the boy's hand and they walked down the hall.

Crawford gazed at Travis. "How's his mother? His uncle didn't know her condition when he called."

"I honestly don't know, either. We're heading to the hospital now and I hope to get some details."

"Good. I gave Levi a snack but he'll still need dinner. Will you make sure he gets something?"

Travis was confused. "Of course. Why wouldn't he?"

The teacher seemed to be choosing his words carefully. "Levi tells me he doesn't always get to eat. He rarely has breakfast, either. Some days I think the school lunch is the only meal he gets."

The comment shocked Travis. "He's thin, but he's not malnourished. I would know if he was." As he said the words, he second-guessed himself. He saw Levi eating maybe two meals a week. *Surely Sam gives the boy breakfast and dinner?* He realized guiltily that Sam was probably in a bigger hurry to get to his house in the evenings than he was to make sure his nephew ate.

"Okay, I'm just repeating what the child has told me. Plus, some days his clothes are dirty. I'm not sure how often they're washed. I don't know how much he bathes, either."

Travis' hackles were raised. "Okay, Mr. Crawford. I'll take all that under advisement. Levi will be cared for, I assure you."

The boy returned with the secretary, and Travis couldn't get him away quickly enough. "You ready, bud? Let's go see your mom and Uncle Sammy."

Levi held his hand and Travis led him out. He turned to the woman and said, "Thank you." He cast another glance at the teacher, then walked out.

Levi chattered about his day on the fifteen minute trip to the county hospital. Travis listened with one ear while his mind raced. Why did he feel so indignant that the teacher had questioned Levi's care? He didn't know what went on in the crappy little apartment the boy called home. It bothered him that Sam was being accused of neglect, because Travis knew that Sam took more care of the child than Melanie ever did. As a pediatrician he should have seen it. Was such unacceptable behavior the fault of Sam or the boy's mother?

He pulled into emergency parking and helped Levi out of the back seat. Again holding his hand, he led the boy into the busy ER. Travis glanced around but didn't see Sam. He approached the front desk. "Sam and Melanie Madison were brought here by ambulance?"

The young woman behind the counter glanced at a clipboard. "She's not able to have visitors but he's in room E-three, just down that way." She pointed to a hallway.

"Thank you." He started to direct Levi when the woman interrupted.

"Children really aren't allowed back there."

Travis exhaled. "He needs to see his parents. There's no one else to watch him."

"Just for a few minutes, then," she relented.

"Of course." Travis headed down the hall. He wasn't sure why he'd called them Levi's parents. Partially true, but the rest of the truth took too much fucking energy to decipher. He paused in front of the doorway to E-three and glanced at Levi. "Uncle Sammy is in here. He might be banged up, okay? Just be prepared."

Levi nodded nervously.

Travis opened the door and looked in. "You decent?"

"Hey!" Sam smiled. "Come in." He didn't look much worse for the wear. His right wrist was swollen and purplish, and there was a knot on the side of his head.

"Uncle Sammy!" Levi ran to him.

"Careful," Travis advised as the child hugged his uncle.

"I'm okay." Sam glanced at him while squeezing Levi. "I'm glad you're here. Sorry we were late. It was a stupid accident."

They were alone in the room, but Travis wouldn't have cared if they weren't. He stepped close to Sam and gave him a hug and a kiss on the temple. "I was so worried. Glad to see you're mostly in one piece."

"I'm fine," Sam assured. With his good hand, he cupped Travis' chin and planted a kiss on his lips.

Travis smiled back, grateful Sam hadn't rebuked his affection. He needed to be close to Sam right then, and it seemed Sam felt the same way. Travis bent down and picked up Levi, setting him on the exam table by his uncle. "What happened, Sam? And what's going on with Mel?"

Sam shook his head and looked away.

Travis spotted tears in the corners of his eyes. He removed a handkerchief from his pocket and passed it over. "Take your time."

Sam dried his eyes and looked over Levi's head helplessly.

Travis understood it was difficult to talk. "Okay," he agreed.

"It just happened so fast. I lost control of the car and it rolled. Mel was knocked out and they took her away before me, although the EMT did say she was stable."

"That's good."

"Yeah. They just X-rayed my wrist to see if it's broken. I've got some bumps and bruises, but that's basically it."

"Thank God," Travis breathed a sigh of relief.

The door opened and a doctor entered. "Mr. Madison? I'm Dr. Kramer."

"Sam Madison." Sam nodded. "This is my – um, Dr. Travis Nelson. And this is Levi." He touched the boy's head.

Travis couldn't tell if Sam was trying to keep their secret so as not to embarrass himself, or to protect Travis. At this point, he didn't care and extended a hand. "I'm Sam's partner, and Levi's pediatrician. Did the films indicate a break?"

Kramer shook his hand. "Dr. Nelson, good to meet you. No fracture, just a capsular sprain of the dorsal wrist." He turned to Sam. "It's not broken, but there is a significant sprain. Fortunately, the alignment is well maintained throughout. I believe we can treat you with a removable brace. You'll want to ice it and keep it elevated as much as possible. If you're in a lot of pain I can prescribe a few days' worth of painkillers, but otherwise just take anti-inflammatories."

Sam shook his head. "I'm okay."

"If you change your mind, tell a nurse before you leave and we'll get you a script. They'll bring you a brace and show you how to wear it."

"For how long?"

"At least two to three weeks. After that I'd expect the pain to minimize and you can wear it as needed."

"I'm not sure I can type in a brace."

"You type much?" Kramer asked.

"Only for a living."

He smiled. "Not for two to three weeks, you won't. I expect you'll have significant pain for at least that long. After that, a minimal amount of typing and some gentle range of motion strengthening exercises for six to eight more weeks. By then you should be in good shape. If not, see your doctor." He glanced at Travis. "Or see this doctor. He can let you know what's normal and what's not."

"I can do that," Sam agreed.

Travis spoke up. "Do you know what's happening with Melanie Madison?"

"Yes." Kramer appeared confused. "I thought she was your wife."

"Twin sister," Sam offered.

"Ah, I see. Melanie has a fracture of her distal radius. She's been taken to surgery for it to be fixed and casted. She sustained a decent crack on the head so we're going to keep her overnight for observation. Provided everything checks out, she can go home tomorrow."

Levi glanced at Dr. Kramer. "She fractured her radiator?"

Travis touched the boy's hand. "Radius, buddy. I'll tell you about it in a minute."

He nodded.

Kramer said, "Thank you. When you're done here, the nurse can direct you to the surgical waiting area."

Travis shook his hand again. "Thank you."

"Thanks," Sam repeated.

Kramer left, and they were alone again.

Sam looked at Travis. "What does Mel have, in English please?"

"A broken arm. The radius is one of two big bones in the forearm, the one on the thumb side. Distal radius means it's closer to her hand than her elbow. They'll take her to surgery and set the bone, then put her arm in a cast. It'll probably stay on for six weeks or so, then it'll come off. She'll be fine as frog hair before you know it."

"Can we see her?" Levi asked.

"Maybe after the surgery, for just a few minutes," Travis said. "Then we're leaving. We're going to your apartment to pack some stuff, and you two are coming to stay with me for a while."

"Yay!" Levi clapped his hands.

Sam shook his head. "Mel won't want that."

Travis shrugged. "Mel doesn't have much to say about it, for tonight at least. We'll deal with tomorrow…tomorrow."

Sam put his head on Travis' shoulder. "Thank you, babe."

"Any time and every time." Travis kissed the top of his head.

Levi glanced at them. "What's a pe'trician?"

"What, honey?" Travis smoothed Levi's curly hair.

"You told my teacher you were my pe'trician. And you told that other doctor, too."

Travis smiled. "Oh. A pediatrician. That's the kind of doctor I am. I take care of children. Like you." He poked Levi in the belly lightly.

Levi glanced at Travis, with his arm around Sam. "I think you take care of grown-ups, too, Dr. Trav."

Travis and Sam exchanged smiles. "Sometimes, Levi. Especially the ones I really care about."

* * * *

Sam paced the floor in the surgical waiting area. It'd been two hours since he'd gotten his brace and they'd discharged him. Now he was waiting for news about Mel.

Travis had taken Levi to the cafeteria to get some dinner. He'd wanted Sam to come along but Sam couldn't think about food. He was too sick to eat.

I should have pulled over when she started the argument. She had the bad habit of bringing up important topics when he was driving, so he couldn't give her his full attention. She'd done it too many times to count in the past. This was the first time he'd ever wrecked the fucking car.

He couldn't fathom she really believed the things she'd said. Had Derek influenced her somehow? Were the drugs addling her brain? He didn't want to think about what might happen when she woke up, if she was still angry with him. She could take Levi and run away, if she thought she had somewhere to go. Since Derek apparently didn't have anywhere to stay, he couldn't believe either of them had a place to run to.

Sam held his head in his hands. He'd thought things were bad a month or so ago, but they'd seemed to get better. How had they gone south again so quickly?

"Mr. Madison?"

He glanced up at a doctor in scrubs. "Yes?"

"I'm Dr. Brown. I operated on your sister. She's going to be just fine. Her arm has been casted, and she's on some pain meds. Hopefully she can sleep tonight. As long as she's stable tomorrow you can take her home."

"Thank you. Can I see her?"

"She's groggy. You can step in for a minute, then she needs her rest." He led Sam to the recovery room and motioned to her bed.

Sam took the seat next to Mel's bed and held her good hand. Both right-handed, they'd each managed to injure their dominant arms. He sighed. *How will she care for herself now?*

Mel's eyelids fluttered before she opened them. "Sammy?" Her voice was hoarse.

"I'm here, sis." He squeezed her hand.

"Where's Levi?"

"He's here, too. Travis took him to the cafeteria to get something to eat."

"Good." She closed her eyes again, then opened them once more. "Really tired."

"The doctor said they're giving you pain meds and you should sleep well tonight."

"Want to sleep," she agreed. "Tell Levi I love him and I'll see him tomorrow."

"Okay. Trav and I are taking him home."

"Would you call Derek and let him know what's happened? He'll be wondering."

Hell no. "I don't know his number."

"It's in my phone."

"I don't have your phone, Mel. It's somewhere in the heap of metal that's now my car."

A tear rolled down her cheek. "I'm sorry, Sammy."

"Yeah, me too. I can call the bar, I guess. They'll tell Derek."

"Thank you." Relieved, she closed her eyes and drifted off.

He sat with her for a few more minutes, then got up and walked out.

Levi sat on Travis' lap in the waiting room. They both looked at him expectantly. "Did you see her?" Travis finally asked.

Sam yawned and nodded. "She's very tired but she's okay." He ruffled Levi's hair. "She said to tell *you* she loves you, and she'll see you tomorrow."

He nodded and put his head on Travis' shoulder.

"We're all tired," Travis offered. "I think we should go pack some stuff to take to my house."

"I've got to find the number of the bar and call her boss." Sam hoped fervently he wouldn't have to talk to Derek.

"I'll help you." Travis stood and carried Levi out.

In the parking lot, Sam wiped his eyes again. "I guess I'll have to call the insurance company about my car. I only had liability, of course, so I'm pretty much screwed."

"We'll figure it out." Travis unlocked his car and strapped Levi in the back.

Sam glanced back at him. "He doesn't have his booster seat."

Travis got in. "And yet, he survived the trip here."

"Is everything always going to be roses and sunshine with you? I need to know, now, because otherwise that's going to piss me the hell off."

Chuckling, Travis started up the car and drove. "Just trying to balance your negativity with some optimism. Things could be worse, Sam. They could be very much worse."

"I don't have a fucking car anymore." Sam knew he sounded like a petulant child, but he couldn't control himself.

"And I told you we'd figure it out. You're not alone, babe. You don't have to shoulder all this by yourself, and it doesn't have to be resolved tonight. For now you need to eat, and then you need to sleep. Both of those will be best accomplished at my place." He pulled up in front of the apartment complex.

"I thought we were going to your house," Levi said, his voice panicky.

"We are, honey. We need to pack a bag for each of you first so you can come and stay."

"Okay."

Sam led them to the door and realized he didn't have his keys. He'd been lucky to walk away from the crash with wallet and phone. He tried the door and found it unlocked, so they went in.

"Unlocked?" Travis blinked. "Are you kidding me?"

He shrugged and turned the lights on. "Levi's room's in there." He opened a closet and pulled out a trash bag. "Here's his suitcase."

Travis snatched the bag. "Classy. Come on, Lev. Let's get your clothes."

Sam took a bag for his own clothes and filled it. He did have a suitcase, and loaded it with other possessions that he wanted to keep. Since neither he nor Mel had keys any longer, he couldn't lock the door. Which meant anything inside was fair game for thieves. He grabbed his computer and all his work notes.

"Jesus H. Christ!" Travis yelled from Levi's room.

"What?" Sam poked his head in.

"Fucking cockroaches!"

Sam wasn't fazed. "And?"

Travis' face reddened. "And... All this shit stays in the garage until I get a chance to wash it. We're *not* bringing roaches into my house."

Sam sighed. "We can stay here, Trav. Levi and I will be fine."

His face grew redder. "You will most certainly *not* stay here! Take everything you want now because, if I have my way, you two won't be coming back."

Sam turned to go back to his room. "Hate to break it to you, dude, but you probably won't get your way." He continued shoving stuff into his bag.

Travis yelled from the other room, "Hate to break it *you, dude*, but I almost always do. Now chop-chop. We're wasting daylight."

Sam could only smile.

At Travis' house, they piled their bags on a workbench in the garage, removing only what they'd need to wear the next day. Sam carried those things and his laptop into the house.

"You need to eat something," Travis insisted. "I have leftover pizza or some frozen dinners."

"Pizza sounds good. And beer. Lots of beer."

"One beer." Travis kissed his temple. "I'm going to stick Levi in the tub then give him a bedtime snack."

"He doesn't usually eat before bed." Sam reheated a couple slices of pizza.

"He can if he wants to," Travis insisted. "The choice is his."

Sam nodded, too tired to argue. He must have zoned out because he was still nursing his beer when a pajama-clad Levi joined him in the kitchen for cookies and milk. When the last drop of milk was gone, he supervised Levi's teeth-brushing and helped Travis tuck the boy into the large bed in the spare bedroom.

He seemed so small in the queen-sized bed, and acted a bit nervous to be left alone.

"I'll leave the hall light on," Travis agreed, "and we'll only pull the door partway closed. Like this. Okay?"

"Okay," he agreed hesitantly.

Sam leaned in for a hug. "Night, Levi. Sleep tight. Love you, kid."

"I love you too, Uncle Sammy." He hugged Sam's neck tightly.

Levi reached for Travis next. "Night, Dr. Trav. I love you."

"Aw. Love you too, buddy. Goodnight. We're right down the hall if you need us."

"Okay."

Travis ushered Sam out and pulled the door closed as agreed. He glanced at Sam. "You want some help brushing your teeth, sweetie?"

"Shut up." Sam shoved him gently and padded down the hall. He entered the master bath and managed to not only brush but also floss with one good hand. It took three times longer than normal and his wrist hurt like hell afterward, but he'd gotten it done.

Sam stripped to his boxers and climbed between the sheets where Travis waited for him. "I'm beat."

"I know. I just want to hold you and count my blessings."

"Fucking optimists," Sam muttered teasingly.

Travis wrapped his arms around Sam and cradled him. "You know you love my sunny disposition."

Sam didn't know anything about anything at that point. He could barely keep his eyes open. "Super tired."

"Close your eyes. Sleep." Travis pressed light kisses to Sam's temple and shoulder. "We'll talk tomorrow. It's Saturday. We can sleep in."

"Have to get Mel," Sam reminded.

"If we remember," Travis teased.

"Not funny." They'd barely remembered to call the bar. Sam had, and had left a message with some bartender. That was all he'd agreed to do. His conscience was clear.

Travis nuzzled his neck and spoke soothingly. "Look, I don't know what happened to cause the accident, but judging by your behavior, I suspect it had something to do with Mel and Mel's boss. For just a second there, I actually wished your sister would have some type of minor setback and be forced to stay in the hospital longer. I know that's horrible and totally against the Hippocratic Oath I took when I became a doctor, but I'm human, too, and sometimes I can't help myself. When Mel hurts you, I want to hurt Mel."

"Need to protect Mel," Sam murmured groggily.

"We'll take care of her," Travis reassured him. "But I'll save my protection for you and Levi. Now relax. Go to sleep. Everything will be fine." He placed a kiss on Sam's ear. "I love you."

Sam's eyes popped open, and wordlessly he closed them again.

Chapter Six

Sam was awakened by something crawling over his feet. In a dreamy state he thought it was one fucking huge cockroach, so when he opened his eyes and realized it was just Levi, he felt relieved. He glanced at the clock. *One a.m.* "What are you doing, buddy?" he whispered.

"I woke up and forgot where I was. I got scared. Can I sleep here with you?"

Hesitating, Sam glanced behind him at Travis. The doctor's eyes were closed but he lowered the covers to welcome the boy in.

Sam smiled. "Sure. Come on, under the covers."

Levi scrambled between them and Travis tucked him in, eyes still closed.

"Can we go to the zoo tomorrow?" Levi asked.

"Probably not." Sam ran a hand through the child's tousled hair. "I'll have to pick your mom up whenever the hospital releases her. She'll want to see you, but she'll need to rest, too."

"No talking at this slumber party," Travis said. He'd yet to open his eyes. "Remember 'slumber' means 'sleep'."

"Go back to sleep, Trav," Sam said softly.

"I'm trying, but you Madisons won't stop talking."

Levi giggled. "Go to sleep, Dr. Trav."

Travis growled and went after Levi, nuzzling his neck until the boy was laughing hard. He draped an arm over the child and rested his hand on Sam's hip.

Sam yawned, and at some point fell back to sleep.

* * * *

When he woke the next time, morning sun streamed in through the blinds. The nightstand clock read seven-twenty a.m. He rolled over and found Travis lying there, watching him. Levi slept peacefully between them. "Hey," he whispered.

"Good morning," Travis whispered back.

"Sorry." Sam glanced down at the boy and back up again.

Travis shrugged. "I'm not. He told me he loves me last night."

Sam smiled sheepishly. "Yeah. Sorry. I'm not saying I *don't* feel that way, but I've got a lot of things on my plate right now."

"I understand." Travis gazed at him dreamily. "I just fucking love you so much, I had to tell you how I felt."

"Thank you." Sam thought the silence between them would be uncomfortable, but it wasn't.

"How's the wrist feel?"

"Hurts."

"I'll bet. You want to tell me what happened?"

Sam sighed. He really didn't, but had to. "You were right. It was about Mel and Derek, her boss." He relayed the story, and the events up until the car flipped over.

Travis winced. "I'm sorry, man. She's totally using you. I guess you can see that now."

"She's my twin sister. Once upon a time we shared the same womb space. How can I *not* let her use me?"

"I don't know, but what she's doing isn't right. You and Levi are staying here, and if you want to, you can take him to visit her after school like you offered."

"Except I no longer have a car. She does."

Travis shook his head. "I'm not sure I want her coming here."

"She's my sister," Sam insisted.

"Sister or not, she's a messed-up drug addict, and you know it. We can meet her on neutral ground or you can take the kid back to the roach motel. But you're not staying there ever again. You got that?"

Sam blinked. "Are you seriously telling me what I can and cannot do?"

Travis held his gaze. "I sure as hell am. If you've got a problem with that, then we'll have to settle this another way. Arm wrestling, maybe?"

Sam laughed out loud.

Travis covered his mouth with one hand to keep from waking Levi. He then replaced the hand with his mouth, and kissed Sam long and hard.

Groaning, Sam slid his good arm around Trav's neck. They kissed for long, succulent and blissful moments.

"I need to pee," Levi announced when he woke. He crawled out from under the covers and scampered off to the bathroom in the hall.

Sam took advantage of the opportunity and pulled Travis on top of him. They ground their hips together as they kissed hungrily. "Have to stop," he finally whispered when he heard the toilet flush.

"One more kiss." Travis dove back in and Sam was lost again.

"Can I watch cartoons?" Levi asked from the doorway.

Sam and Travis froze, gazing at each other.

"Sure," Travis replied. "The remote is on the coffee table. Pull the door shut, okay? I'll be out in a couple minutes to make pancakes. Maybe we can let Uncle Sammy rest just a bit longer."

"Okay." Levi closed the bedroom door.

They continued to stare at one another until they heard the sound of cartoons coming from the living room TV.

Travis crouched down under the covers and planted himself between Sam's legs.

"I thought I was supposed to be resting," Sam teased.

"You are. I'll do all the work." Travis drew Sam's cock into his mouth and sucked until he was fully aroused.

Sam gasped at the incredible feelings which were waging war with his guilt. *We shouldn't be doing this with Levi in the house.* On the other hand, his friends who were parents joked constantly about sneaking around for sex when they could manage a minute without the kids. Saturday morning cartoons were a huge favorite among them. He and Travis weren't so different.

Or am I simply trying to justify my actions because I'm so horny I can almost feel the orgasm closing in? Either way, he wasn't about to ask Trav to stop. His lover sucked until Sam felt his balls draw up. At that point, Travis climbed on top and clutched both their cocks in one of his hands. He stroked them together, the delicious friction causing a new, amazing sensation.

"Aw, God," Sam muttered.

Travis leaned in for a kiss, swallowing further moans. "Come on," he coaxed as he jacked them off together.

"Now!" Sam ground out as he shuddered.

Trav groaned and released at the same time, two hot streams of cum coating the both of them. He kept up his ministrations until they were both sated, then returned to kissing Sam with as much heat and intensity as he'd ever known. "God, I love you," Travis murmured. "And I love making love to you."

"I can honestly say I love that, too," Sam admitted.

Travis grinned. He climbed out of bed and grabbed a towel to wipe his stomach, hands and groin area.

Sam watched his handsome hunk slip into jeans with no briefs and carefully raise the zipper to avoid pinching anything important. Travis then slipped into his shirt from the day before, leaving it unbuttoned. "I'll go make breakfast and shower later. How about you? Sleep some more or shower?"

"I'll shower. Thanks for…you know. And thanks for making Levi's breakfast."

He grinned. "No problem. I like to…you know. And I like to cook." He tossed the towel to Sam. "I'll let you stick that in the hamper. I've got mountains of laundry today anyway."

Sam sat up. "You don't have to wash all our clothes. They're clean."

"Humor me." Travis winked and left the room.

Using the towel, Sam cleaned himself up then rose and headed to the master bath to shower. His wrist was tender and he tried not to bend it but that was easier said than done. It was almost a relief when he could dry off and put the brace back on. The compression made it feel better.

He dressed and joined Travis and Levi in the kitchen eating pancakes. "Hey, those look good." He pressed a kiss to Trav's temple and another to the top of Levi's curly hair.

"They are good." Levi's praise was genuine.

Sam couldn't remember the last time he or Mel had fixed pancakes. He didn't know why, either. They weren't that difficult.

Travis stood and grabbed another plate. "How many would you like?"

"A couple, please." He sat on the other side of Levi and accepted the plate, along with butter, syrup and orange juice. "Wow. A feast."

"Uncle Sammy, Dr. Trav has chattoos! Can you see them?" He pointed to Travis' open shirt, and the inked skin beneath.

Travis made a face. "Sorry," he mouthed.

Sam waved him off. "No big deal," he mouthed back, then said aloud, "I see them, Levi. Aren't they cool?"

"I want a chattoo," Levi decided.

"You can have as many as you want," Travis agreed. "You just have to do one thing. The same thing I did."

"What?" Levi's eyes shone.

Travis leaned in nose to nose with him. "Wait until you're twenty-five, and you know what you want to do with your life. After that, you can decide about getting tattoos."

"Okay." He scraped the last few bites off his plate then looked at Sam. "Are we going to get Mommy today?" Levi had syrup dripping from his chin.

Travis used a napkin to dab the boy clean.

Sam could only smile at the both of them. They were cute as hell together. "That's the plan."

Travis said, "You might want to call first and make sure she can come home. If for some reason she can't, there's no need to take Levi all the way over there."

Nodding, Sam fought back the worries creeping in to his mind. He had to voice one of them. "I don't even know how I'm going to get her."

"I'll take you, of course. We'll have to share my car for a while but we can make it work."

"Well, thanks." Sam didn't know what else to say. The offer was extremely generous. He finished eating then called the nurses station at Cook County Hospital. The shift nurse told him Melanie would be able to go home later that morning.

Travis had loaded the dishwasher than started the first load of Levi's laundry.

Sam joined him. "She can go around eleven," he announced.

"Fine." Trav didn't look at him, just kept sorting. "We'll leave at ten-thirty, then. Pick her up and drop her at the apartment."

Sighing, Sam folded his arms across his chest. "How can I leave her there all alone? She has a broken arm for Christ's sake. She needs help."

"Says the man with the severely sprained wrist? I don't know, I think the better candidate to help might be the boss who's scrounging for a place to stay anyway."

"I don't know him," Sam replied flatly. "Other than he's a stoner, and she's my sister, Trav. I can't *not* help her."

"You *are* helping her. You're taking care of her most prized possession. Would she rather lose Levi to Child Protective Services?"

"What are you talking about?"

"Levi's teacher told me he's been coming to school dirty, with dirty clothes. And Levi has mentioned that he doesn't get much to eat at home. They were pretty concerned about him."

Sam frowned. "Crawford said that? I saw him a couple of days ago. He never mentioned anything to me."

Travis shrugged. "It's a delicate subject, but teachers are mandated reporters, just like doctors. Eventually they would have reported Melanie and both of you would have lost him."

"Son of a bitch," Sam muttered. *When it rains, it pours.* "I don't know how much more I can handle."

"There's nothing to handle here, babe. I've got you and Levi under control. The three of us are good. We just need to figure out how to help your sister without compromising any of us."

Sam narrowed his eyebrows. "Meaning what, exactly?"

"Meaning I don't care if you want to help her, but you and the kid are staying here. That's not up for debate."

"But she's not welcome here?"

"Not if she's going to smoke cigarettes and use illegal drugs. I won't have those things in my house. If she thinks she can stop all that, we might be able to talk. But I don't give warnings, babe. She breaks the rules or lies, and she's out."

The rules were suddenly overwhelming Sam. He couldn't resist snipping, "My, aren't you the supreme dictator?"

Travis shrugged. "My house, my rules. If she wants to make my house payment, I'll let her have a say." He leaned in and kissed Sam's mouth. "Now, I'm going to hop in the shower, get dressed, and cover up my 'chattoos'. I forgot, and I thought Levi's eyes were going to pop out of his head."

Sam smiled. "Kind of like the first time I saw them."

"Oh, hell no. Your eyes were popping for a different reason, sailor. The minute you saw them, you wanted to swab my decks."

"I still do." Sam waggled his eyebrows.

"There's always tonight. You live here now, remember?" Travis winked and headed for the shower.

"Hey," Sam called after him.

Travis paused and looked at him. "Yes?"

"I was thinking about getting a tat. Do I have to wait until I'm twenty-five?"

His lover looked surprised. "How much longer is that?"

"December twenty-fourth. Mel and I were Christmas eve babies."

Travis thought about it, then shrugged. "Yep. Have to wait." He continued down the hall.

"Bossy!" Sam called after him. He rubbed his hands over his biceps to ward off an imaginary chill. *Is he really bossy, or just self-confident?* Travis seemed to be able to handle all the balls Sam felt like he was juggling. He wasn't entirely comfortable with Travis telling him what to do, but he knew his lover's heart was in the right place. And for now, having someone to guide him, someone he could lean on, felt like such a relief. He could live with bossy, especially when it came in the sexy form of Travis Nelson.

* * * *

Travis buttoned his long-sleeved shirt and left it untucked over his jeans. He thought about Sam as he tugged on socks and tied his shoes. He needed to tread lightly, but it was so damned hard.

His mom had called him bossy once as a boy, and they'd had a good-spirited debate about it. He didn't see how he could be called bossy when he was right. His mother had tried to explain the complicated theory of perception. Other people didn't automatically see things the same way he did.

He recognized that in the argument Sam had had with his sister just before the accident. Sam thought he was bending over backwards to help Mel. She thought *she* was the one helping *him* by giving him a place to live.

Her argument was bullshit, of course. She was taking complete advantage of his good nature and soft heart. She might not want to admit it, but she had to know it.

Travis didn't have a sister, let alone a twin, so he didn't quite get their sibling connection. He just knew what he'd observed, and that was Mel using Sam for her own purposes. Travis wouldn't allow himself to be used. If she thought she was going to say what he wanted to hear, that she'd stop smoking and using drugs, and he'd automatically believe her, well... She had another think coming. He'd believe that when he saw it.

He cared for Sam and Levi, though, and knew he needed to try to care for Melanie. He'd suggest they stop so Levi could pick out flowers to take to the hospital for her. It wasn't much, but it was a start.

When they arrived at the hospital later, Levi was strutting as proud as a peacock, carrying the bouquet into her room.

"It's about time," Melanie spouted. "I'm going nuts here. I need a smoke in the worst way."

"I picked you out these flowers, Mommy." Levi offered them to her.

"Aw, thanks, little man." She tossed them on the tray table next to her bed. "Sammy, where are my clothes? I need to get dressed and maybe that'll hurry the nurses along."

Travis couldn't believe she'd barely acknowledged the gift. Levi was gazing at her, seeking a smidgen of approval, and she was jonesing for a smoke. His blood boiled.

He placed a hand on the boy's shoulder and squeezed.

Sam opened the closet and found a bag with her things inside it. "Here they are, I guess. They're not in great shape."

Mel snapped her fingers and reached for the bag. "Whatever, we're just going home. You may have to do some laundry. I obviously can't do it."

Travis cleared his throat and mumbled, "Derek," at the same time.

Sam caught his message. "Maybe Derek can do your laundry. Has he moved in yet?"

She looked at him snippily. "Well, I wouldn't know, now, would I? He hasn't called or dropped by. Did you phone him like I asked?"

"I called the bar, yes."

"Stupid son of a bitch," she muttered, and tried to untie her hospital gown, which was tied at the neck. "Help me out here."

Sam went to her side and loosened the tie.

Mel looked at Travis and sneered, "You want to avert your eyes?"

He grabbed Levi by the shoulders and turned them both away. "I absolutely do. Come on, Levi. Let's wait in the hall until your mom is decent." He led the boy out, muttering, "Of course, that could be a very long wait."

The boy glanced up at him. "Do you think she liked the flowers, Dr. Trav?"

"Sure she did! Your mom is so anxious to get out of here, she didn't say much. But once she gets them home she'll put them in a pretty vase so she can enjoy them all week."

A strange look crossed Levi's face. "Are we going home to the apartment? Or home to your house?"

Travis squatted so he could face Levi. "You and Sam are coming home with me. I don't think your mom would enjoy that very much, so we're going to let her stay at the apartment. She might have a friend come to help her out. But don't worry, you'll get to see her every day after school. Sam and I will make sure of that."

Levi smiled. "Okay!"

Is that relief on his face? Travis could have sworn the child's concern was more about leaving his house than missing Melanie.

Sam opened the room door. "Come on in."

Levi reached for Travis' hand and they returned to Mel's bedside.

"Are you in much pain?" Sam was asking her.

"Off and on. They gave me some good shit, it knocked me right out. Gotta make sure they give me a script for that." She glanced at Travis. "I guess you could always write me one, couldn't you?" Melanie smiled, but there was no mirth in it.

He gazed at her evenly. "Sorry. I only prescribe for my patients."

"Oh that's right. You're not a *real* doctor," she sneered. "You're a *pediatrician.*"

"He's a real doctor!" Levi insisted.

Travis squeezed his hand.

Sam looked at the boy. "Of course he is. Mom is teasing."

The nurse came in with paperwork for Melanie to sign, along with her obviously important prescriptions. Twenty minutes later she was free to go. Sam helped her into the obligatory wheelchair and placed the flowers in her lap. Clutching the bag with her things, he wheeled her out. Travis and Levi followed behind.

"We'll bring the car around," Travis offered, and took Levi with him to the parking lot. As he buckled the boy into the back seat, he commented, "We need to get you a proper booster seat. We'll have to do that later today."

"What happened to my other seat? It was in Sam's bug."

"Good question, Levi. Sam should probably see if there's anything salvageable from his Volkswagen." He got in and drove to the entrance where Sam and Mel waited with the nurse.

Sam opened the front passenger door for Mel.

Travis hopped out and opened the rear door. "Here you go. You'll want to sit back here with Levi."

Mel had started to climb in the front. She looked at him pointedly and moved to the back.

Travis closed the door for her. He returned to his seat.

Sam thanked the nurse who took the wheelchair and went back inside before he got in the front. He glanced over at Travis. "Thanks."

Reaching for his hand, Travis squeezed it. "You bet. Let's get Mel home."

She said, "You don't have a booster seat," to Levi. Leaning forward, she muttered, "You should know that he needs a car seat."

"We'll get him one today." Travis glanced at her in the rear-view mirror.

"It doesn't matter, he won't be riding in this car again." She glanced around. "Though it is pretty snazzy. What's a car like this cost?"

He couldn't believe her tactlessness. "About three times what a bar waitress earns in a year," Travis replied.

Sam's eyes bugged out and he shot Travis a look.

Travis shrugged and whispered, "It was a rude question."

Sam let it drop, and apparently so did Mel. They rode to the apartment in silence.

Travis pulled to a stop in front of the complex.

"Hope everything is all in one piece," Sam commented.

"Why wouldn't it be?" Melanie asked.

"Because I don't have any keys, so I had to leave the place unlocked last night." Sam turned to Travis. "We really need to find my car and see if I can get my keys back. I had some stuff in the trunk, too. Not sure if I'll be able to get it out."

Mel added, "My keys and phone were in the console by the gear shift."

"We'll look for them," Sam agreed. "God knows where they ended up."

Travis nodded. "I'll make some calls, and see where your car was taken. Hopefully we can go look at it today. It won't be pretty."

"No doubt." Sam sighed.

They got out of the car and filed into the small apartment.

Mel picked up a black leather jacket from the sofa. "Looks like Derek was here."

"Made himself right at home," Travis muttered.

She frowned at him. "He was invited."

Travis stared right back. "Good. Just so you know, Sam and Levi have been invited to stay with me. So we'll be leaving soon."

"I don't think so." Mel shook her head.

Sam stepped forward. "Yeah, we will. It's just for now, Mel. You can't take care of Levi with a broken arm and this'll give you a chance to heal. We'll do what needs to be done, and I'll bring him to see you after school. Every day, if you like."

"I don't like. I don't like it one bit."

He sighed again. "Look, it was your idea to bring Derek here. It'll be too crowded with all of us. This is the perfect opportunity to give everyone some much-needed space."

She appeared resigned, but still not happy. "Who's going to fill my prescriptions?"

"I'll do it." Sam rifled through her hospital bag and pulled out two slips of paper.

"Do it today. I'll need those painkillers."

"I know," he answered dutifully.

She dropped onto the sofa. "If I let you take him, you'll have to bring him back whenever I want. You got that?"

"I got it." Sam sounded deflated.

"And none of this 'we're too busy right now' crap. My son is the most important thing in my life."

"I know," Sam repeated.

Travis had heard enough. He picked up the bouquet Melanie had tossed on the coffee table and asked Sam, "Is there a vase we can put these in? The most important thing in her life picked these out and I promised him we'd put them in some water when we got here."

"Sure." Sam opened cupboards until he found a juice pitcher the appropriate size. "This'll work."

Travis removed the outer plastic wrap from the flowers and stuck them in the pitcher, then added water. He set them on the coffee table in front of Melanie.

She reached out and grabbed his arm. "I don't like your attitude."

Travis gazed at her levelly. "Right back atcha, sister. You might want to remove that hand before we have to see about getting you a second cast."

She released her hold but continued the menacing stare. "You're a big talker. Do you have the balls to back up your threats, cake boy?"

Sam jumped. "Mel, stop it! You've never used such derogatory slang about me before, why would you do it to Travis?"

Travis held up one hand. "It's okay. I'm going to chalk this up to the pain meds and her head not being in the right place at the moment." He tried to pierce Mel with his icy stare. "Make no mistake about this. You'll understand the true meaning of a threat if you slur Sam or me again. Like it or not, I care about him and I won't stand by and watch you continue to push him around."

Her face contorted in anger. "Sam and I share blood ties. You have nothing to say about our relationship. And I don't 'push him around'. We do things for each other."

Sam muttered, "What have you done for me lately?"

Travis smiled.

"You need to get out!" Mel screeched. "Both of you! Go! Now!"

Travis grabbed Levi's hand. "We're going. Say goodbye to your mother, Levi." He headed to the door before the child ever had a chance.

"Don't you take my boy! Come here, little man. Stay with Mommy."

Travis paused and looked at her. "He's not a 'little man'. He's a child who needs love and attention. At this point in your life, I don't believe you're capable of providing either." He glanced at Sam. "We'll be waiting in the car. Come on, Levi." Travis led him out.

"Come back here!" Melanie yelled.

Tightening his grip on Levi's hand, Travis kept walking. When he reached the car he stopped and knelt to look Levi in the eye. "I'm sorry you had to see that, sweetheart."

Tears streaked the child's face. "I was afraid you might leave me there."

"Not today, buddy. I know you love your mom, but she's got some problems right now and they need to be worked out before she can care for you properly." He brushed the tears away with his thumbs.

Levi sniffed. "I don't like it when she yells and uses bad words."

"I know, and I'm sorry about that, too. Lots of adults yell and use bad words, but we shouldn't do it in front of our children. It's a hard thing, because we get caught up in the moment sometimes."

Levi slid his arms around Travis' neck. "Can we go home now?"

Travis hugged him close. "Pretty soon. We have a few stops to make first."

Sam joined them and Travis rose. "Everything okay?"

His lover nodded. "For now, anyway. I think I got her calmed down. I told her we'd bring something for her to eat when we came back with the meds."

Travis cupped Sam's neck and pulled his face close for a kiss. "You're a good man. Let's get going, then. We've got a list of stops ahead of us."

Chapter Seven

Sam inspected the twisted hunk of orange metal that used to be his car. "What a mess."

"That's putting it mildly. We're lucky you escaped with only the sprained wrist." Travis took a step closer. "Stay back, Levi. There's lots of broken glass." He peered in where the driver's window had once been. "Your keys are still in the ignition. Let's see if they'll come out." He reached inside carefully and managed to pull them free.

"Great." Sam breathed a sigh of relief. "Do you see Mel's keys or phone anywhere?" He gazed in through the passenger window.

"They could have been ejected when you rolled. Wait! I see something." Travis pried the door open as far as it would go before squeezing inside to snag another set of keys. "Her phone's on the floor on your side. If you can get that door open you should be able to reach it."

Sam wedged the crumpled door open enough to retrieve the phone. "Good. This'll make Mel happy."

Travis stood and dusted off his jeans. "My one goal in life."

Sam shot him a look and proceeded to the front of the car. "Now, if I can just get the bonnet open."

"What's a bonnet?" Levi asked, following along.

"The front hood of a Volkswagen. See, most cars have the engine in front. This one has the engine in the back, where the trunk should be. The trunk here is under the bonnet." He unlocked it and opened the hood. His toolbox was intact and he pulled it out. There was a bunch of other crap that he'd forgotten about which suddenly seemed important. He loaded his arms with it until they were full.

Travis stepped next to him and touched a cardboard crown from a fast food restaurant. "Is this really vital?"

Tears filled Sam's eyes. "Yes, damn it. *It's mine.* I want what's mine."

"Then by all means, we'll take it. Anything else?"

Sam checked out the trunk. *Empty.* Like the void in his heart when he thought about his car. "No."

"Okay, then." Travis slammed the bonnet and led Sam to the back of his car. He opened the hatch. "Stick it in here and we'll sort it out at home."

Sam shoved everything in until he was only holding the paper crown. He wiped his eyes and turned to Levi, placing the crown on his head. "There you go, buddy. It was probably for you to begin with."

"Thanks!" Levi laughed.

Travis pulled Sam into a hug and whispered in his ear, "I know how hard this is. I'm here for you, babe. Levi and I will always be here for you."

Great, gulping sobs overwhelmed him and Sam had no choice but to let them out. Travis held Sam tight and allowed him to cry on his shoulder.

"I'm sorry," Sam finally said when the blubbering had stopped.

Travis pulled a hanky from his pocket and dried Sam's face. "It's okay, sugar. Let it out."

"This was my first car. The only one I've ever had. I saved up for it in high school. My uncle, my mom's brother, helped me pick it out. Uncle Johnny was the closest thing to a father we had, and he loved this car. He knew how to work on it, and got it in great running shape." He drew a shuddering breath. "He died, but I still had the car. I didn't know how to fix anything, but found a guy who did. Then mom died, but I still had the car her brother had loved. Parts were getting harder to come by. It leaked more oil than it used, and the brakes squealed. But it reminded me of my uncle, and my mom."

"I'm sorry." Travis ran a hand through Sam's curls. "You'll always have those memories, Sam. The sentiment isn't replaceable but the car is. We'll find you another vehicle. Maybe even something from this century," he teased.

Sam tried not to smile and shook his head. "I can't think about that now. It's all too much. My insurance won't pay since I only had liability, so I'll be starting over with no money for a down payment. I'm screwed. I may have to borrow your bike."

Travis chuckled. "My bike probably cost more than this car. Don't worry, we'll figure this out in time. There's no rush. We can manage with the one vehicle for a while." He leaned in and kissed the side of Sam's head before whispering in his ear, "Whatever I have, I'll gladly share with you. Car, bike, penis, tongue… Anything you want, you got it."

Sam laughed out loud and his spirits lifted. "There you go, channeling Roy Orbison again. Thank you. I don't know how I'd manage without you right now."

"You don't have to find out. Now come on. Those scripts are probably ready, and Mel's no doubt getting hungry."

"She'll be relieved to see her phone."

"Anybody would be. We'll get her some food and after, we'll stop at Mario's for the pizza buffet. What do you think about that?" He glanced at Levi.

"Yay!" the boy cheered.

Sam could only smile. Travis already knew the way to cheer him up was to mention pizza and penises. He adored both.

After taking Mel lunch and her drugs, they went to Mario's and ate until Levi was stuffed. Next was shopping for a new booster car seat. Finally they stopped at the grocery store to pick up what Travis called 'supplies for the week'.

Sam had never seen so much food loaded into a shopping cart. As they strolled down each aisle, Travis asked Levi what he liked and added items to the cart. Sam stopped joking about what he liked because Travis added all those things, too. He tried putting some of them back on the shelf but Travis wouldn't let him.

"Humor me," was all Travis would say. He paused in front of a cheese display. "Do you like these, Levi? They'd be good to pack in your lunch." He held up a package of individually wrapped, low-fat string cheese.

"He eats lunch at school," Sam said.

Travis made a face. "School lunches are high in fat and sodium. They're okay occasionally, maybe once a week. But we can pack a more nutritious lunch for him to take on a regular basis."

Sam bit his lip. He'd need to speak with Travis. It was okay to dote on Levi for a while, Lord knows the kid could use the attention. But getting him used to something that couldn't continue was another story. There was no way Mel would pack a lunch for him each day.

The Lexus was loaded when they finally rounded the corner to Travis' house. Sam saw a motorcycle in the driveway, with two riders wearing black leather jackets. For an instant he thought it might be Derek and Mel, and he panicked. As they got closer he realized it wasn't them. Mel didn't know where Travis lived, anyway. "Who is that?" he asked.

"Oh wow." Travis grinned. "It's my mom and dad." He pressed the garage door opener on his visor and the big door opened. His parents glanced around and waved when they saw the SUV.

"Wonder what they're doing here?" Travis mused as he pulled into the garage, then hopped out. "Hey! What's going on?" Opening the back door, he lifted Levi out and took him by the hand to go greet them.

His folks parked the bike and climbed off. "We were just leaving," his mom said. "We thought we missed you."

"Just out taking a spin," his dad replied.

Sam eyed the handsome couple who were very obviously related to Travis. His father had the same closely cropped brown hair, with just a touch more gray. His three-day beard also had shades of white streaked through it. And the dark eyes that looked so much like his son's had just a few more smile lines around the edges.

His mother was also attractive, with shoulder-length brown hair, bright eyes and an infectious smile.

"I'm so glad you're here." Travis released Levi long enough to kiss his mom and give his dad a quick hug. "I'd like you to meet my friends. This is Sam Madison and his nephew Levi. Sam, Levi, these are my parents, Kim and Dave Nelson."

Levi shrank back behind Travis' leg but Sam stepped forward and extended his hand to Kim. "Pleasure to meet you, ma'am."

She squeezed his hand. "You're sweet but there's no need to 'ma'am' me. I'm Kim. The big guy is Dave." She waved a thumb in the direction of her husband.

Sam offered his hand to Dave and they shook. He had a firm grip and a warm smile. "Sam, happy to meet you."

Kim squatted in front of Travis and Levi. "Hi there. You must be Levi. I'm Kim."

He gazed at her warily. "Are you Dr. Trav's mom?"

She smiled up at Travis. "I didn't know anyone else called you that." To Levi she said, "Yes, I am. Dr. Trav is my baby, but he's also a very good doctor. His daddy and I are quite proud of him."

Levi seemed to think about that. "He has chattoos, you know."

Kim glanced up at her son questioningly.

He opened his collar to expose some ink.

She caught the meaning. "Oh! Tattoos. He sure does. More than one man needs, I'd expect."

Levi looked at her. "Did he get in trouble for getting them?"

"No. He's a grown man. I just joke about him still being my baby."

"I'm gonna get a chattoo," Levi announced.

"Not until you're much older," she insisted.

Travis chuckled. "No worries, Mom. We've already had the discussion. No 'chattoos' until age twenty-five... For Levi *or* Sam." He looked at his lover and winked.

Sam's heart melted, but he couldn't respond because the parents were now staring at him.

"How old are you?" Kim asked Sam straight out.

"I'm six," Levi replied.

She turned his attention to him. "That's great! You're just finishing up first grade, then?"

He nodded.

"Dave and I are both high-school teachers. He teaches math and English is my field."

Levi gazed up at Travis with some amazement. "Your mom and dad are teachers?"

"Yeah." Travis fingered the boy's curls. "It sounds a lot neater than it is when you don't get your homework done, and you have to face your parents not only at school, but then again at home!"

"Wow," Levi mouthed.

Sam thought the discussion had taken the spotlight off him, and his age. He'd yet to ask Travis how old he was, the subject just hadn't come up. But Sam figured he was in his early thirties.

"Back to the subject at hand." Kim faced Sam. "How old did you say you were?"

He swallowed. "Twenty-four."

She looked at Travis. "Cradle robber."

He laughed. "You're just jealous. Sorry, he's taken. Besides, you wouldn't want to break Dad's heart." Travis clapped his hands. "Now, I'm really glad that you're here, because we have a carload of groceries and Sam should not be lifting with his sprained wrist. If I sweet talked you two into helping me unload, would you consider staying for dinner?"

"You don't have to do that," Dave said. "Of course we'll help."

Levi said seriously, "We're grilling hamburgers and hot dogs."

"That sounds yummy," Dave told him.

Sam opened the hatch of the car. "Then stay. We bought enough stuff to feed an army and a half."

Kim glanced at the car loaded with bags. "Oh my. We might have to stay so I can help organize this miniature grocery store."

Travis reached for some bags and handed them to her. "And laundry, Mom. We have a mountain of Levi's laundry." He mouthed, "Cockroaches."

She accepted the bags and nodded. "I'm a whiz at laundry, but that means you'll have to feed me. And there'd better be some ice cream in all these bags."

Sam hoisted a load with his good hand and headed inside. "Three different flavors. Travis wanted to please everybody."

"He always does," she sighed.

Sam and Kim began unpacking while Levi ran back and forth and the other men did the heavy lifting.

Kim chatted as she spread things out on the counter. "What do you do, Sam?"

"I'm a freelance writer for an online company. People pay me to write fresh content for their blogs and websites."

"Seriously. I had no idea there was such a job."

"I get that a lot. It's a good gig. Pays well and I can set my own hours. Which is nice considering I can't type for a couple of weeks."

"What happened?"

"Car accident. My sister broke her arm. That's why we have Levi with us."

Kim seemed familiar with the kitchen as she began putting things where they belonged. "You must be close with her, to help her out like this."

"We're twins," he admitted. "About as close as siblings can get, I guess. Oh, that sounded bad. Didn't mean it to." He felt his face flush with heat.

She waved him off. "I think it's nice. Travis never had any sisters or brothers. I feel rotten that he missed that experience, but it just wasn't meant to be."

"He would have made a great brother. He's very caring and supportive."

"A bit *too* much, at times," she said.

Before Sam could inquire what she meant, Travis, Levi and Dave carried in the last load and closed the door.

"This is it," Travis announced. "I'm just going to start another load of laundry, then I'll be back to help."

Dave glanced over the food. "Good Lord! What, is he stocking up for winter?"

"Or maybe a growing boy." Kim shot her husband a knowing look.

Sam suddenly felt very uncomfortable.

Travis' return made it better. He obviously loved his parents and they adored him. They laughed and chatted as his mom helped with the laundry and his dad grilled the meal. The atmosphere at dinner was casual and friendly. Sam relaxed a bit and could tell Levi liked the Nelsons.

After the dishes were done, Sam slipped away to phone Mel and make certain she was doing okay. He wasn't sure if he was relieved or not that Derek was there. At least she wasn't alone.

When he returned, Travis had helped Levi into his pajamas and they were brushing his teeth. He glanced at Sam. "We found a library book in Levi's backpack, and my mom's going to read him a story."

"It's early." Sam glanced at his watch.

"He's beat, Sam. He was falling asleep during ice cream. He's had a busy couple of days."

"Okay." He watched his nephew curl up to Kim while she read two stories to him. He didn't nod off but was very close to it.

When she'd finished, Travis scooped him up and carried him around to say good night. He tucked Levi in bed and came back to tell his parents goodbye.

"Thank you," Sam told Kim. "He enjoyed that."

"He's a delightful little boy."

"It was great to meet you," he told her and her husband.

"You too, Sam," Dave said.

To his surprise, they each gave him a quick hug. Sam watched them go as Travis saw them out.

He thought he'd check the garage to make sure all the lights were out, but when he stepped out he realized the door was still open and he could hear Travis speaking to his parents.

"That child is becoming attached to you," Kim said.

"I know, and the feeling is mutual. He's a really good kid, Mom."

"I can see that he is. That's not the point. What's going to happen when his mother is able to care for him again? Going back to the dingy little apartment you described will be hard for Levi—not to mention tough for you to let him go."

"I'm not sure his mother will ever be able to care for him. She does drugs and God knows what else. Sam might have to consider suing for custody."

Sam blinked rapidly, stunned. He'd never once considered that option. Obviously, Travis had. And when had he described the 'dingy little apartment' to his parents? Sam hadn't heard.

"Just be careful, son," Dave said. "Don't get your hopes built up."

"I'm trying to stay positive."

"Which is good, but you have to protect yourself."

Kim added, "And don't let your heart get broken again."

"I'll be careful." Travis gave both of them hugs.

Sam slipped back into the house, thoughts and emotions swirling around in his head. He paused in the doorway to Levi's room and watched the boy sleep.

Travis had already considered the idea of Sam going for custody. The thought was almost laughable. Travis was the good parent, the responsible one. Sam had been the one who'd sent Levi to school in dirty clothes, and unwashed. He'd fed the kid at the normal times but had never bothered to ask if he was hungry at other times. He couldn't take care of Levi forever. The thing was, Mel wouldn't need him to. She'd be fine soon, and want him back.

"Hey." Travis slipped in behind him. "He's beat. I'll bet he sleeps all night."

"He enjoyed your mom reading to him."

"She's great, isn't she? What'd you think of my parents?"

"Amazing," he replied truthfully. "Very cool."

"They are." Travis sighed. He brushed the hair away from Sam's neck and placed a kiss there. "So… The boy is asleep and we're alone. Seems like we should make the most of this time, don't you agree?"

Sam had more trouble switching gears than Travis evidently did. Thoughts and phrases from the evening were still lingering in his mind. Yet the longer his lover nuzzled, the more responsive Sam became.

Suddenly, *not* thinking seemed like the medicine he needed. And Travis Nelson was just the physician to fill his prescription.

Travis captured Sam's good hand and tugged so his lover would follow him. He led Sam down the hall to the bedroom where he closed and locked the door.

"Levi," Sam whispered.

"Is sound asleep, but if he wakes he can knock on the door. We don't need him walking in on us."

"Of course. You think of everything."

Travis smiled. "I certainly try. Right now, all I can think about is sucking your cock. Why don't you strip out of those clothes so we can get started?"

"No need to ask me twice." Sam wasted no time peeling away his things. He removed the brace and laid it on the dresser.

Travis eyed him as he undressed. "How's the wrist feel?

"Not bad. The brace helps."

"If I get carried away, remind me that it's still sore." He picked up the sprained hand and placed light kisses on Sam's skin. "Still swollen. That should go down in a few days. It's starting to bruise."

"Good, because purple is such a lovely color on me."

Travis waggled his eyebrows. "I agree. I enjoy your cock when it's engorged and throbbing. The head turns a magnificent shade of purple."

"You sure know how to sweet talk a guy."

Leaning in, Travis sucked a spot behind one ear. "I know how to fuck a guy, too. Lie down on that bed so I can suck and fuck your brains out."

Doing as requested, Sam tossed back the covers and dropped to the mattress. "You planning to do all the work again?"

Travis climbed between his legs. "I thought I might. You did an awful lot of running around today, for someone who's supposed to be taking it easy."

"I'm okay."

"Yeah, you are. Now lie back and relax, and we'll see if I can make you feel better than okay."

Closing his eyes, Sam smiled. "I have no doubts."

Travis began kissing one ankle and worked his way higher, kissing, licking and sucking as he went. When he reached the apex he skipped the good parts and made his way back down the other leg. Sam's toes were perfectly shaped with neat, little round toenails. Travis had never had a foot fetish, but something about these feet, right now, called to him. He sucked a toe into his mouth and laved it like a miniature cock.

Sam twitched and shuddered each time he focused on a new toe. By the time he'd reached the tenth, Sam was moaning. "God, Trav! Who knew toes could be so erotic?"

"Yours are driving me crazy, man." Travis hated to move on but Sam's cock was standing tall and proud and already leaking pre-cum. The creamy ribbon was too luscious to ignore.

He kissed his way higher and licked the swollen cockhead before sucking it for a moment. Travis kept going, licking his way up taut abs to circle each flat nipple. They puckered and hardened with the attention, and he couldn't resist sucking one in his mouth while twisting the other between two fingers.

"Damn, baby!" Sam groaned. "You're pushing all the right buttons tonight."

"Such a sexy stud." Travis continued his ministrations as Sam stroked his back with a light, feathery touch. "I just want to eat you up."

"Start with my cock, please," Sam teased.

Travis chuckled. "Impatient boy. That's okay, I'm ready for it, too."

More slick pre-cum coated the crown and Travis was ready to give the shaft proper attention. Lowering his mouth over the tip, he licked the salty seed before allowing the staff to ease down his throat.

"Aw, God!" Sam thrashed on the bed.

Travis pulled out long enough to murmur, "Tastes so good. Gonna suck you hard until you come, and I can swallow every drop. Then I'm gonna spread your legs and fuck your hot, tight ass."

"Yes, please." Sam bucked his hips, encouraging Travis to take more.

"Mmm, baby." Travis bobbed his head up and down over the shaft, making slurping sounds as he mouthed the cock. "Wanna taste your cum."

"Keep that up and it won't be long."

He fondled Sam's balls and could tell when they drew up into tight orbs. Sucking one finger into his mouth, he circled it around the edge of Sam's hole before pressing it in to one knuckle.

Sam gasped and bucked his hips wildly.

"Mmm, somebody wants to be fucked," Travis teased.

"God… Yes!"

"Come for me, first, then I'll get right on that. Or should I say, I'll get right on *you*." He cackled a sultry laugh.

"I'm close," Sam gritted his teeth.

Travis slurped and sucked with abandon, fingering his lover's hole and balls alternately.

"Now!" Sam grunted and hot, steamy spunk gushed from his cock.

Wave after wave filled Travis' mouth and he swallowed every drop.

Sam bucked and thrashed until his load was spent, then fell back onto the bed, panting.

Travis swiped the back of his hand across his mouth as he rose and reached for a condom and lube. As he rolled the latex over his shaft he said, "I was thinking that you and I each ought to get one more blood test, then we could lose the biohazard suits."

Sam opened his eyes and gazed at Travis. "Sounds good to me. Lose it now if you want. I trust you."

"Nah, I can wait. Decisions made in the heat of the moment often aren't smart ones."

"You're such a Boy Scout," Sam teased.

"With over a hundred tattoos. Right." Grinning, he greased his shaft then inserted the slick finger into Sam's ass. "Just for that I'm not using much lube."

"Bring it on, man. I'm ready and waiting for whatever you've got to offer."

He pulled the finger out and nudged his cock to the opening. "Ready for this?"

"Absolutely." Sam bucked his hips.

Travis pushed forward until his cockhead popped in. Sam groaned.

He paused. "Hurt?"

"Hurts so good, baby. Don't stop. Fuck me like you promised."

With a satisfied growl, Travis plunged forward until he was balls deep in the ass he'd become so familiar with. "Nice and tight," he groaned. "Damn, I love burying myself inside you."

"Feels incredible from this angle, too. Fuck me, Trav. Fuck me hard and fast. Make me forget about everything but your gorgeous face, and your hot cock reaming my ass."

"My pleasure." He drove deep, again and again, pounding away at the demons hounding his lover.

"There's nobody but you and me, Sam. Look at me. Ride this wave with me." He clutched Sam's once-again engorged shaft and jacked it in time with his thrusts.

Sam gazed into his eyes.

Travis panted and grinned. "You and me, baby. It'll always be you and me. I love you, Sam. Damn, I love you."

Sam didn't blink. "I love you too, Trav. I've never felt for anybody what I feel for you right now."

Travis' heart soared as an intense climax washed over him. He growled and shattered, shooting his seed in pulsing waves.

He continued to grasp Sam's cock and soon it erupted with semen coating his hand and their stomachs. "Fuck, aw fuck," he muttered.

Sam reached up and drew him into the circle of his arms. He placed light kisses on Travis' face and soon they were kissing, tongues entwined. The kisses were salty sweet. One of them was crying. Travis couldn't be sure it wasn't both of them, and he didn't care. "I love you," he repeated again.

"I love you, too," Sam murmured between hungry kisses. He cupped Travis' face with both hands. "I love you so much it fucking hurts."

Travis pulled back and grinned. "Sure you do, right now. Let's see if you can say it with your pants on."

They cleaned up and Travis checked on Levi before calling it a night. The boy was sleeping soundly. He returned to bed and spooned behind Sam, who was already breathing steadily. Happier than he'd ever remembered being, Travis closed his eyes.

When he opened them much later, Sam had shifted positions and was staring at him. "Hey." He rubbed his eyes. "What time is it?"

"Midnight."

"Can't sleep?"

Sam shook his head.

Travis sighed. He twisted one of Sam's curls around his finger. "What's bothering you, babe? Worried about Mel?"

"A little. Worried about Levi, too. Just plain worried, I guess. I, uh, didn't mean to, but I heard you talking to your parents in the driveway tonight."

"Oh." Travis tried to recall what they'd been talking about.

"Who broke your heart?"

Travis blinked. "Excuse me?"

"Your mom mentioned someone who broke your heart. Who was it?"

"My last boyfriend, Jack. It's been over for a while, now. But it was painful."

"How long were you together?"

"About three years. He drank. It wasn't a drinking *problem* at first, but it ended up that way. I just couldn't handle it anymore."

"I'm sorry."

Travis shrugged. "All roads led me to here, and I wouldn't trade what I have now for anything."

Sam smiled but pressed on. "Your mom said Levi's growing attached to you. You told her the feeling is mutual."

"It is. What I *didn't* tell her is that I love you, and that feeling is mutual, too."

"I do love you, Trav, but it's too soon. We're getting too comfortable here. Levi will be lost when I uproot him back to the *dingy little apartment*."

"Then don't do it. Nobody's asked you to leave."

"Now you're living in a fantasy world. Mel's going to want him back, and I guarantee you it'll happen sooner rather than later."

"Mel has a lot of work ahead of her. She needs to clean up her act before she can even think of getting Levi back. I told you, it's not just me saying this. The teachers at school noticed it, too."

"What's pathetic is you suggesting that I might need to go for custody. I'm not a fit parent, Trav. I don't know the first thing about raising a kid."

"Sure you do. Besides, we'd be doing it together."

"But..." Sam looked down, then up into his eyes again. "How can we consider including him in our lives when we don't even know what we have, yet? Awesome sex isn't enough to build a relationship on."

Travis blinked. "Is that all you think we have? I think we have a really special friendship in which we enjoy spending time with one another. We have an amazing camaraderie, we care for each other, we make each other laugh, and yeah, we make each other horny as hell. So are you kidding me? We know what we have. We both know. Look me in the eyes and tell me you don't know."

"And we have a six year old who may or may not be a permanent part of our family. Can you live with that, either way? If Mel decides to marry Derek and move Levi to Nantucket, we'll have nothing to say about it. He belongs to Mel. Are you cool with that?"

"Nantucket? Where the hell did that come from?"

"Rhymes with 'fuck it', which I seem to be saying a lot these days. Answer me, Travis. Are you interested in me? Or are you more interested in me and Levi as a package deal?"

Travis squirmed uncomfortably. "Of course I want you, but I want Levi to be taken care of as well. It doesn't have to be mutually exclusive."

"No, but it might be out of your hands, my friend. You may have to go along with whatever decisions someone else makes. Can you accept that?"

Bullshit. He said, "Of course," but Travis was really thinking, *We'll see.* He traced one finger across Sam's cheek. "Don't think so hard, babe. We don't have to solve all the world's problems tonight."

"I know." Sam smiled sheepishly. "But if we could just solve one, I might sleep better."

Travis drew Sam into his arms. "I'm sorry, sugar. Is there anything I can do to help?"

"Yeah. Let me count your tattoos? You said you have over a hundred."

"No need. I have one hundred and twelve. Some of those are smaller ones combined into larger pieces, so they'd actually be hard to count."

Sam kissed Travis' jaw. "Okay, so maybe I didn't really want to count them. Maybe I just want to lick them, and rub my cum into them. Or rub your cum into them. Probably both. Would that be okay?"

Travis flopped onto his back. "I suppose. If you must." He caught Sam's eye and winked.

His lover opened his mouth and went to work.

Chapter Eight

Sam pulled into the parking lot of Jefferson Elementary School and nudged his car into one of the few available parking spots. He still wasn't quite comfortable driving something bigger than his Beetle, but he was happy to have *any* car. The dark green Ford Escape wasn't *that* much bigger, but took some getting used to nevertheless. The price had been right, though. He'd felt lucky when Travis' mom had decided she wanted a new car, and had sold him her old one for a few thousand dollars.

They'd signed the deal two weeks ago, about a month after the accident. His wrist twinged occasionally but was basically healed, and he was back to writing full time. Mel had recently gotten her cast removed, and Sam was living on pins and needles waiting for her to ask for Levi back. So far she'd been preoccupied with Derek.

Sam had finally met him and the guy hadn't seemed so bad. Of course he hadn't come right out and *asked* Derek if he was a drug dealer, but Sam suspected he was. Mel still looked lit most days when he saw her.

The whole situation filled him with impending dread and he walked around on edge, waiting for the ax to fall.

Mel had promised to meet him at the school for Levi's first-grade promotion and end of year program. The coming summer brought a new crop of problems for Sam, who hadn't quite decided how he'd take care of Levi and manage to work, now that he was busier than ever.

He made his way toward the auditorium and looked around the crowd of parents in the hallway. *No Mel.* He spotted Travis and his mom, and weaved through the throng to join them. "Hey."

Travis' eyes lit up like they always did when he saw Sam. "Hey there!" He leaned in and pressed a kiss to Sam's cheek.

"Hi, honey." Kim kissed him next.

Sam smiled. He was used to the affectionate family by now. "Glad you both could make it."

"Dave sends his regrets, there was just no way. I have a planning period this hour, but I'll have to skip out if this runs long."

"I don't have much more than that," Travis agreed. "But we wanted to be here."

Sam glanced around again. "Any sign of Mel?"

"Nope." Travis picked a string from the sleeve of his shirt. "You really think she'll show?"

Sam shrugged. "I guess we'll see."

"We should go in," Travis suggested. "We don't want to have to sit in back."

"Okay, but I'm saving her a seat." Sam moved toward the auditorium doors, where Levi's teacher stood.

Colton Crawford smiled at them. "Well, hello. Good to see you. I was hoping you'd be here so I didn't have to phone you."

Sam gazed at him. "Is something wrong?"

"No, I just wanted to tell you that Levi's turnaround the past few weeks has been amazing. He seems happy and outgoing. Physically, he appears to be thriving."

"Good." Sam breathed a sigh of relief. Travis might have fond memories of getting called out in front of teachers like his parents but Sam's memories weren't that humorous.

Travis spoke up. "I think we've got a good handle on things now. Thanks for your help."

"Anytime. Did you get a chance to check out the summer camp program we talked about?"

Sam looked at Travis. "Summer camp?"

Travis cleared his throat. "I was going to mention it to you. Can we talk about it tonight?"

"Sure." Sam wondered exactly what there was to talk about. Levi was too young to go away to camp. He'd never agree to it and neither would Mel.

"Enjoy the program," Crawford said.

"Thanks." Sam led the way in, choosing seats near the front on the outer aisle. If Mel arrived late, she could slip in that way. He sat next to the empty chair and Travis sat beside him, with his mother on his other side.

Travis leaned over and squeezed his hand. "Sorry, babe. It came up rather quickly and I hadn't found time to mention it yet."

"No problem. I'm not sending Levi away to camp, though. I don't think he's old enough, and Mel will never agree."

"No one is sending him away. It's a day camp. Monday through Friday from eight to two. He'd need to pack a lunch and a couple of snacks. The kids take swimming lessons daily, and get to experience a bunch of other activities and crafts. There's even a trip to the zoo scheduled one day."

Kim added, "I've heard it's a great program."

Sam nodded. "It sounds pretty good."

The principal stepped on stage and welcomed the family members.

"We'll talk more tonight," Sam agreed.

Travis squeezed his hand and held it.

When the principal finished his welcome, the first-grade students filed on stage and stood in rows on bleachers. The music teacher stepped forward and the kids began to sing.

The song was nearly over when Mel breezed in and slipped into the chair next to Sam.

He glanced at her and was shocked at her appearance. Her hair was wild and unkempt. Her dirty jeans were shredded in several spots. The tank top she wore was not only stained, but it exposed too much cleavage and a butt-ugly shoulder tattoo he'd never seen before. Sam figured it was supposed to be a pixie or fairy of some kind, but it looked more like a blue toad.

"Hey," he whispered.

"Hey." She fidgeted nervously. "Where is he?"

"Second row, third from the left."

She searched for him and nodded. "These things are so lame."

"They mean a lot to little kids, though." He remembered how excited Levi had been to invite them. He'd asked to call Kim and Dave himself, even though Travis had warned him they'd be working so not to get his hopes up. Sam had had to remind him to invite Mel. He'd felt guilty that night, realizing Levi was becoming less and less attached to her.

He glanced at Mel's shoulder again. "When'd you get the tat?"

"Isn't it cool? A friend of Derek's did it."

"Toad?"

She swatted his leg. "Fairy."

"You calling me a name?"

Mel laughed out loud and he grabbed her arm and squeezed to silence her.

"I'm getting one, too," he said. "As soon as I decide on the design I want."

His sister gazed at him skeptically. "You? I'm surprised the minister would allow you to do such a thing. Oh I'm sorry, I mean the *doctor*."

Sam bit back a chuckle. "Yeah, he was pretty pissed when I told him I wanted one. But I stood my ground. I told him that I'm my own man, and if I want to get a tattoo then damn it, I'm going to."

"Good for you." She nodded.

Travis leaned forward and looked at them. "You're missing a good program."

"Sorry," Sam whispered.

His lover glanced casually at Melanie. "Hey, Mel."

"Travis," she acknowledged, then turned her attention to the stage.

When the kids were finished they came down into the audience with a long-stemmed carnation for each of their parents. Levi's face lit up when he spotted his family and approached them. He gave one flower to Travis and one to Sam, then smiled at Kim. "I told them I needed three."

Sam gulped. He knew Levi hadn't noticed Mel, but she sure as hell had seen what he'd done and was winding up to bitch.

Kim pressed a kiss to Levi's forehead and said, "Thank you, sweetheart, but I'll bet you didn't see your mother sitting down there on the end. You should give this to her." She handed the flower back.

Levi glanced at Mel and Sam saw honest-to-God fear in the boy's eyes. He approached Mel and held the flower out. "Hi, Mommy."

"Hey, little man!" Mel gave him a hug and accepted the carnation. "For me? Thank you!" Her voice was high pitched and exaggerated.

Sam wanted to sink under the floor and he suspected the rest of his family did, too. It dawned on him that for the first time ever, he'd lumped Travis, Levi and Kim under the 'family' category but excluded Mel. The realization made him more uncomfortable than his sister's phony tone.

They exited to the back of the auditorium where the school had supplied refreshments. Levi had a cookie and Mel took three, wrapping them in a napkin and shoving it in her pocket. "You want to come home with me, little man?"

The frightened look appeared in his eyes again. "Uncle Sammy promised me we could get ice cream."

She shot Sam a dirty look. "You can get ice cream any time, can't you? I never get to spend time with him anymore."

He shook his head. "Not my fault. I've offered to bring him by every day after school. You're usually busy."

Mel glared at him. "Well I'm not busy today. School is out soon, so I'll be able to spend a lot more time with him."

"Has your schedule changed?" Travis asked.

She looked at him. "Excuse me?"

"Has your schedule changed? We were under the impression that you worked evenings until late and slept all morning."

"No it hasn't changed," she snapped at him. "But Sam's will have to. Levi needs something to do all day."

Sam spoke up. "We're thinking about enrolling him in day camp. He'd go from eight to two each day. They offer swimming lessons and lots of other activities."

"That can't be cheap. I hope you're not expecting me to pay for part of it."

Sam could see Travis bristle at the remark. He set his jaw and replied, "When have we ever asked you to pay for anything? We've got it, Mel. We think it'll be a great experience for him."

"It might be. *If* I choose to allow it."

Sam sighed. "Please, Mel. You'll have to sign the permission forms, I'm sure."

She smiled evilly. "Then I guess you'd better stay on my good side. Levi, are you sure you don't want to come home with me? We could stop by the convenience store and load up on junk food for dinner. Anything you want."

"Dr. Trav says eating too much junk food isn't healthy."

She rolled her eyes. "*Dr. Trav* is such a prig. Whatever, kid, it's your loss. See you soon, little man." She turned to walk away, tossing her carnation on the floor as she went.

"She is one piece of work," Kim muttered softly.

"What's a prig?" Levi repeated.

Travis squatted to face him. "Kind of like a goody two shoes. And you know what? That's not the worst thing I've ever been called." He grinned.

Levi laughed.

Travis continued, "That was an amazing program, Levi. Thanks so much for inviting us. I've got to go back to work for a couple of hours. I'm going to find a vase for my beautiful flower so all my patients can see it."

Levi hugged him tightly.

"Love you, buddy."

"I love you too, Dr. Trav."

He stood up. "I'll see you tonight. Don't eat too much ice cream because we'll probably go back out and get more later." He waggled his eyebrows.

"Okay!" Levi grinned from ear to ear.

Travis hugged his mom. "Thanks for coming. Maybe we'll see you this weekend?"

"You bet. Take it easy."

He moved in front of Sam and slipped one arm around his waist, then drew him close.

Sam grinned. "You think this little PDA is a good idea in front of a school full of potential patients and their parents?"

Travis shrugged. "It's no secret that I'm gay. Anyone who has a problem with it can find another pediatrician. They won't find one as happy as I am, though." He pressed a kiss to Sam's mouth.

Heart fluttering, Sam savored the kiss before it ended too soon. "Same goes, baby. Have a good afternoon."

Travis winked at him, ruffled Levi's hair, and left.

Kim smiled at Sam. "I raised a good one, didn't I?"

Sam laughed. "Totally. I *so* owe you for that one."

Levi piped up, "We could take you for ice cream."

She crouched down to his level. "I wish I could, buddy. I have to go back to work, too. Your program was so good. I can't wait to tell Dave all about it. He'll be sorry he missed it. We'll see you soon, though. Have fun on your last few days of school!"

He gave her a hug and she squeezed him tight.

Kim stood and hugged Sam. "See you soon."

"Thanks. See you." He smiled at her as she left. They'd become friends over the past six weeks and he respected Travis' parents a lot. It was clear that Levi was smitten as well.

He reached down for the boy's hand. "Do you need to get anything before we go?"

"My backpack is in my classroom. You can see our dinosaur bulletin board."

"Dynamite! Let's hit it." They walked to the room and Sam checked out everything the child wanted to show him. It occurred to him how easy Levi was to please. All it took was a few moments of attention, speaking to him at his level, listening to what he had to say. Small things, sure, but they deeply impacted the child's self-esteem. He wondered why Mel couldn't see it.

Walking hand in hand from the room, they ran into the teacher again. Sam smiled. "Great program, Mr. Crawford. We enjoyed it."

"Please, call me Colt. Most of the credit goes to Mrs. Weaver, the music teacher, but the kids were amazing, weren't they? They all worked so hard."

"You should be proud." Sam squeezed Levi's hand. "I know we are."

"And I know Levi is a lucky young man. I'm sorry we're just getting to know each other now that the year is coming to a close. I think you, the doctor and I have a lot in common." He grinned.

Sam wasn't sure how to respond.

Colt covered his mouth. "Oh good grief, I didn't mean that like it sounded. I was talking about friendship, and an interest in ink. I believe we have a mutual friend, Eddie Ortega?"

Sam shook his head. He hadn't heard the name.

"Oh, I figured you knew him. He's the tattoo artist who's done most of Travis' ink. He's done all of mine, too."

Sam blinked. "You have tattoos?" He noticed for the first time that Colt was wearing long sleeves, like Travis always wore in public.

Colt nodded. "Almost as many as Travis, or so I'm given to understand from Eddie. I've never seen his of course, but I'd like to someday."

"I'm sure he'd feel the same way. Maybe we can get together for a drink or dinner some night with you and your partner." He glanced down at Levi, remembering that he and Trav had other obligations now. Yet full-time parents did it. Surely he and Travis could find a way to make it work. "Give me your number and we'll see what we can work out this summer."

They exchanged cell numbers and said goodbye. Sam walked Levi out, intrigued that Colt also had a body full of ink and he'd yet to get even one. The tattoo itch was niggling at him again. He'd have to choose a design soon.

Levi chatted as they walked. He changed subjects at least four times and finally asked, "Does Mr. Crawford really have chattoos?"

Sam chuckled as he unlocked the Escape. "I guess so. Cool, huh?"

"Yeah. Prolly not as cool as Dr. Trav's, though."

"Probably not, kiddo." He tossed the backpack on the seat, buckled the boy in, then headed for ice cream.

* * * *

Travis clutched the bed sheets as his world was rocked. Face down, ass in the air, being pummeled effectively by the guy he loved, he couldn't imagine being any more content.

"Oh yeah." Sam leaned over him, rubbing a hand over Travis' back. "These are the eyes I see in my dreams."

Chuckling, Travis turned his head to speak. "Not mine?"

"Oh, yours too. But these leopard eyes, right here, are usually the last thing I see before I shoot my wad deep into your hot ass. It's a conditioned response thing now. Just looking at them makes me feel good." Sam sucked his back and Travis knew he'd zoomed in on the tattoo of the black leopard.

"Mmm, okay. I see how it is. When you and the cat have finished getting it on, wanna reach underneath and take care of me?"

He sucked harder until Travis squirmed. "Just for that, I gave the cat a hickey. And yes, I would love to take care of you." He slid his hand over Travis' belly and gripped his aching erection. "Every day, for the rest of my life."

Sam jerked in time with his thrusts and continued licking Travis' back. "It's all your fault I'm suddenly into bestiality. Not that I'd want anything to do with a real animal. But this guy back here is part of you, so that's not too twisted, is it?"

Travis groaned as happy sensations came at him from both directions. "No, man, you're totally sane. You can kiss my cat all you want, just don't stop everything else you're doing!"

"Never-gonna-stop," Sam muttered, staccato, as he fucked with intensity. "Come on, big boy. Spill your seed for me. I'm ready when you are."

Another hard thrust sent him over the edge. "Now," he ground out and released. His spunk shot over Sam's hand and the sheets, but he didn't care. The payoff was totally worth it.

Sam's hot seed filled his ass and warmed him from the inside. His lover panted and groaned and Travis felt happy, inside and out. As was his usual MO, Sam clutched Travis' belly and rolled them to one side, away from the wet spot. His lover nuzzled his neck and massaged warm cum into his inked skin.

"Damn, you feel good. I could wake up like this every day."

Travis sighed. "You have a standing invitation. Never have to ask." He turned his head so they could kiss. "Love you," he murmured into Sam's mouth.

"Mmm, love you too."

Footsteps in the hallway gave them just enough notice for Sam to toss the covers over their bodies.

Levi ran in and jumped on the bed. "It's my first day of camp!" he squealed.

Travis grinned at the boy. "Good morning. Not excited or anything, are you?"

"Yes!" Levi bounced on his knees, rocking him and Sam, who were still joined.

"Good morning, buddy." Sam ruffled his hair. "Why don't you go to the bathroom, then change into the clothes we laid out."

"I'll be out in a minute to make you breakfast," Travis added.

"Pancakes!" Levi jumped off the bed and ran down the hall, leaving the door open.

"Maybe, if you settle down!" Travis called back. He glanced over his shoulder and smiled. "Good morning."

"Very good morning." He eased his cock from Travis' ass and threw the covers off. "These sheets are a mess. Guess I'll be doing laundry today."

"Totally worth it," they said at the same time, then gazed at each other and laughed.

Travis showered then made pancakes and ate a quick breakfast with his family. Nearly late for work, he grabbed his satchel and planted a kiss on Levi's head.

"Have fun today, buddy. I can't wait to hear all about it tonight."

Levi wiggled sticky fingers at him. "Have a good day."

Grinning, Travis backed away.

Sam stood and wiggled his fingers in the same manner. "Mine aren't syrupy."

"Then get over here." Travis slid an arm around Sam's waist and kissed him firmly. "Can't wait to see you tonight, either." He lowered his voice. "And if you want to kiss the cat, I'm totally up for it."

"You know I will." He gave one more passionate kiss, tracing his tongue along the seam of Travis' lips.

Travis groaned. "Hate to stop but need to get to work. Have a good day." He pulled away regretfully and smiled over his shoulder. "Sorry about the extra laundry."

"No you're not!"

He chuckled and headed out. "You're right. Call me after you pick him up."

"Will do. Running by Mel's first, though."

"Have fun with that." He winked and closed the door behind him. He drove to the office and looked over the morning schedule the nurse provided. It was busy, but that made the day go quickly.

At lunch he texted Sam some dirty suggestions while he ate a salad in his office, and prepared for his afternoon appointments.

When his cell rang at three he was between appointments so he stepped into his office to take the call. He confirmed it was Sam and answered, "You calling me or the cat?"

"Travis." Sam's voice was hoarse and breathy.

Something's wrong. "What is it?"

"Mel swallowed a bottle of pills. The EMTs are taking her to Cook County now."

His heart thudded in his chest. "Oh my God! What's her condition?"

"I don't know. She's alive but unconscious. We can't be sure what time she did it, how many oxys were in the bottle, or what other drugs were in her system."

Panic turned to rage. "Jesus Christ, Sam! How could she do this to you and Levi? How is he? Is he okay?"

"He's in shock. He doesn't really know what's happened. We have to get to the hospital but I wanted to call you first."

"Where the hell did she get oxycodone, anyway?"

"When she broke her arm, remember?"

"I can't believe she had any of those left."

"I don't know. I've got to go, Trav."

"I'm on my way, babe. I'll meet you at Cook County."

"Thank you." Sam ended the call.

Travis took a deep breath then let it out. An uneasy feeling was forming in the pit of his stomach. Somehow, Mel's actions were going to cause problems for the happy little family routine they had going. He could tell from Sam's tone that his lover wouldn't be happy again for a long time.

He spoke with the doctor on call in his office and arranged for them to transfer the rest of his schedule to his. Travis was out of the door in under ten minutes, and used his hands-free phone to call his parents as he drove.

"Hey, honey." His mom sounded cheerful.

He was about to dampen that mood. "Hey, Mom. Listen, Melanie swallowed a bottle of oxycodone and they've rushed her to Cook County Hospital. Sam and Levi found her, they followed the ambulance. I'm on my way to meet them."

"Oh dear God! What can we do, Trav?"

"Could you come get Levi? He doesn't need to be there."

"Of course. Dad and I will leave now."

"I don't know when I'll be able to pick him up. I'll just have to call you."

"Well, why don't we keep him overnight? We can swing by your place and pack a bag for him, then take him to camp in the morning."

"Mom, that would be amazing. I should be there for Sam, for however long he needs me. It could be a long night."

"It could be a bad night, honey. She might not make it."

"I'm well aware. I'm anxious to get there and find out her condition. Sam was pretty shaken and didn't get many details."

"Okay. We'll see you soon. Drive carefully."

"You too." He ended the call and worried the rest of the way to the hospital.

Travis parked in the lot next to Sam's car and jogged into the emergency room. He spotted Sam in the waiting area, rocking Levi in his arms. Both of their faces were tear-streaked. He thought for a moment that his heart might break. He hurried to them. "Has something else happened?"

Levi bolted from Sam's arms into Travis'.

Sam shook his head. "No news yet."

Travis breathed a sigh of relief. He hugged Levi and sat in the chair next to Sam, running a hand through the child's hair. "I'm so sorry, honey. Are you doing okay?"

Levi didn't reply, just sobbed quietly into Travis' neck.

He reached for Sam and wrapped one arm around him. "Come 'ere. I'm so sorry, Sammy."

Sam buried his face into the other side of Travis' neck and his tears broke loose. Travis held them both and rocked gently, letting each of them cry it out.

When his parents arrived a few minutes later, Kim ran a hand over Levi's back.

He glanced up and saw her, and reached out. She lifted him and sat with Dave in another set of chairs.

"Any change?" Dave asked Travis.

"No news yet. I haven't had a chance to speak with anyone."

A nurse joined them. "Mr. Madison?"

Sam wiped his face and rose. "Yes?"

"Your sister is stable for now, but not out of the woods. We've pumped her stomach but it's nearly impossible to tell how many pills she took, or what else she may have ingested. Those unknown factors are why we can't say she's past the worst of it yet."

"When will we know?"

She shook her head. "Tomorrow morning, maybe? It's hard to say."

"What are we hoping for? I mean, what's a good sign?"

"That she wakes up," Travis offered.

The nurse nodded. "And if she does, that there's no brain damage."

"Brain damage?" Sam's face fell. "Temporary or permanent?"

Travis shook his head. "There's no way to tell this soon."

The nurse glanced at him.

He smiled. "I'm a doctor. Sorry."

"No, it's fine. You can decipher some of this for him, then. It gets overwhelming."

"Can I see her?" Sam asked.

"Not just yet. She's still in the ER. Once they feel she's adequately stabilized, they'll move her to the ICU. Then two people at a time can sit with her. No children, though. Sorry."

"It's fine, thank you." Travis said, and watched her walk away. He turned to his parents, who'd been listening. "You guys might as well go. We just need to hang out and wait, now."

His father stood. "We'll swing by your place, then take him home." He lifted Levi from Kim's arm and she rose.

"Are you hungry, Levi?" she asked. "We should go home and make dinner."

"Wanna stay with Dr. Trav!" He cried, reaching out for Travis.

Travis' heart melted. He grasped the boy's hands but didn't pick him up. "Honey, Mom and Dad are going to take you to their house tonight. You can sleep in my old bedroom. That'll be cool, won't it?"

His tears started again.

Travis leaned in to him and pressed their foreheads together. "I know, buddy. We'll miss you, too. It's just for one night. Uncle Sammy and I need to be here to take care of Mommy. I know this is scary and sad for you, but Mom and Dad will be there for you all night. If you need them, just say something."

He sobbed, "I wanted to live with you, but I didn't want her to die!"

"She's not going to die!" Sam snapped. He scrubbed his hands over his face, fighting his own tears.

Travis pressed a kiss to Levi's cheek. "This is not your fault, honey. It's not Uncle Sammy's fault, and it's not my fault. I can't say exactly what's going to happen, but I promise you that you'll be okay. You are loved so much, and we will always take care of you."

Kim wiped the boy's tears. "We should go. You'll see Trav tomorrow."

"Okay," Levi finally agreed.

Sam gave Levi a quick hug before Travis' parents took him home.

Travis watched them go, then turned to Sam. "I meant every word of that, you know. None of this is our fault."

"Are you fucking kidding me?" Sam gazed at him with disbelief. "Of course it's my fault. I took her son from her. She felt abandoned and alone."

"No, Sam." He shook his head firmly. "Mel made her own choices and she had to live with them. She wasn't alone, but she didn't seem to get that. Ultimately, she chose Derek and the drugs over her family."

Sam dropped back into a chair. "Ever since Rob went to prison she's been floundering. I knew it, I just couldn't seem to turn it around."

"She has a history of bad choices, babe."

Sam's face reddened. "You don't even know her! You'd probably be just as happy if she died!"

Travis flinched. He inhaled and blew out the breath to remain calm. "You don't believe that. I understand how upset you are and, baby, I don't blame you. I've tried to be supportive of your relationship with Mel, even when I could see it wasn't healthy. But she needs help. That's what this was, a cry for help. Good Lord willing, maybe this is what it's going to take to get her the assistance she needs."

Sam stared at him. "She fucking tried to kill herself. Why did she do that, Trav? Didn't she know how much Levi and I loved her?"

"People who are suffering from depression don't think about things like that. They just feel pain, and want it to stop."

"Depression? She was fine."

"Put the pieces together. Levi's dad went away, which upset her. She started using drugs and got in with a bad crowd. It all adds up."

Sam rocked back and forth. "Oh God! Oh God! I'm so stupid! Why didn't I see any of that?"

Travis pressed his forehead to Sam's temple. "Quit putting yourself down. You don't have experience with this and you didn't realize what the warning signs were. This is not on you."

"Levi and I are all she has, Trav."

"No, you're not. She has me, too. And in case you didn't notice, my parents are pretty hands-on people. She has them, too, if she'll just open herself up to being helped."

The nurse returned. "She's being moved to an ICU room. You can sit with her in there if you like."

"Good." Sam rose.

Travis started to follow, but spotted his mom returning with a take-out bag. He approached her. "Hey."

"We brought you a couple of sandwiches. Any change?"

"She's being moved to the ICU. We're going in to sit with her."

"Good. That's something." She handed over the food. "Call anytime if there's news, it doesn't matter what time it is."

He kissed her cheek. "Thanks, Mom. Is Levi doing okay?"

"He's better." They squeezed hands and she left.

Travis caught up with Sam and the nurse at the door to Mel's room. "Can we have this in here?" He held up the bag.

"Sure." She ushered them in, then pulled the sliding glass door closed. "I didn't want to mention this before in front of the little boy, but your sister has some bruising and vaginal tearing. Since she's unable to tell us what happened, we did a rape kit, just to be safe."

Sam went to Mel's side. "Rape?"

The nurse shrugged. "Until she can wake up and tell us if she had rough, consensual sex or not. We'll hold the kit in case we need to turn it over to the police so she can press charges later."

"Thank you," Travis told the nurse.

She nodded and walked out.

Travis pulled the two chairs in the room next to her bed. "She looks pretty good, considering. Rape is... Wow. Not something I'd considered."

Sam didn't seem to want to talk about it. "She looked pale and clammy earlier. God, Trav, I thought she was dead when we arrived, and there I was with Levi. It was awful."

"No doubt. I'm so sorry, babe."

They sat quietly for a while. Travis finally said, "Are you hungry? We have sandwiches."

"Nah. Go ahead."

Travis ate and checked messages on his phone. Sam didn't move, didn't budge from Mel's bedside.

"I'm going to stretch my legs and wash up," Travis told him. "I'll be right back."

Sam nodded absently.

He took his time, throwing away his trash and using the restroom. He washed his hands and splashed water on his face. It was going to be one hell of a night.

He returned to find Sam holding Mel's hand, talking softly to her. "Don't leave me, Mel. Levi and I need you. We love you. *I* love you more than words can say."

Travis' heart ached.

Sam continued, "You're the other half of my heart. You complete me. I don't know who I am without you in my life."

A tear rolled down Travis' cheek. He'd written similar words recently, to Sam, when he'd been practicing how he was going to propose to him. That plan was probably out of the window now.

Chapter Nine

Sam could not believe how badly he'd failed Mel.
When their mother had died, he'd assumed the role of
caretaker, and had felt the responsibility of being there
for his sister. Looking at her now, lying in the ICU bed,
he knew he'd done a fucking miserable job of it.

She'd held her own all night long and seemed to be
resting comfortably. He sincerely hoped that was a
good thing.

He rose and paced around the small room. At some
point Travis had fallen asleep, leaning forward over the
foot of Mel's bed. It looked horribly uncomfortable and
he expected his lover to wake at any minute with a
backache, if nothing else.

Sam paused behind him and ran one hand over his
smooth back. He caressed his shoulders and started
kneading them, massaging gently.

Travis stirred and sat up. He rubbed his eyes and
glanced at Mel. "Any change?"

"Nope."

He stood and stretched, then faced Sam. "Did you
sleep at all?"

Sam shook his head.

Travis sighed and reached for his hips, drawing him close. "She's holding on. That's something." He rested his forehead on Sam's shoulder.

Sam sighed. "I know. I just feel wired up. I wish the doctor would come in. They said he'd make rounds soon."

"He will. Waiting is the hardest part." He curled one finger under Sam's chin and raised it, then pressed a kiss to his lips.

Sam kissed him back. At another time he'd easily have sank into the embrace and desired more. Just now, his emotions were so conflicted he could barely manage the kiss. "You should go so you're not late for work."

Travis shook his head. "I'm not going in today. I'll call one of my partners and my nurse. They can juggle my schedule one more day."

Sam frowned. "There's really no need, Trav. You can't do anything here."

"Being with you is doing something. I love you, Sam. I don't want to be anywhere else."

"Thanks for the thought, but you'll go stir crazy if you're cooped up in here much longer."

Travis smiled. "You know me that well, huh? I'll be fine."

Sam wasn't convinced. "You've given up so much for us already. You don't get to take your daily bike rides anymore. Hell, the last few weeks you've been lucky to get one in on the weekends."

"Do you hear me complaining? It's my choice. Besides, I'm getting my exercise in another manner these days, and you don't hear me complaining about that, either." He patted Sam's hips.

The door opened and a doctor came in. "Good morning. I'm Dr. Evanston, the hospitalist."

Travis released his grip and stepped forward to shake hands. "I'm Dr. Travis Nelson. This is my partner, Sam Madison."

Evanston shook hands and glanced at the chart. "The patient's brother?"

"Yes." Sam moved next to them. "How is she?"

"Her lab results look good today, considering the amount and type of drugs we found in her system."

Travis added, "We never heard what you found, other than the empty oxycodone bottle."

He glanced at her chart again. "High levels of oxy mixed with cocaine, heroin and methamphetamines."

Sam couldn't believe his ears. "Metha-what?"

"Speed," Travis said.

"And heroin?" Sam gaped. "Isn't that the opposite of speed? Why would she take all of them at once? And don't you have to inject heroin? I've never seen any marks on her arms."

Evanston went to Mel's side and uncovered her arms. He glanced at them closely and pointed. "See that? Track marks. Not many, so maybe it wasn't a regular thing for her."

Sam ran a finger over the mark on her inner elbow. "Or maybe she wasn't trying to kill herself. What if she got stoned and didn't realize everything she'd taken? That could happen, couldn't it?'

The doctor replied, "It's doubtful when there's an empty pill bottle like that. The amount in her system indicates she took more than a couple of pills. We just don't know if it was before or after her alleged attack. Only Melanie will be able to fill in those blanks, and that's if she remembers. Regardless, when she wakes up we're required either to admit her for a three-day psych hold, or to release her to a treatment facility. But she won't be free to go home."

Sam thought about that. "How long are the programs in the treatment facilities?"

"Minimum of thirty days."

Travis said softly, "Might be just the thing she needs."

"She won't be happy," Sam murmured.

Evanston shrugged. "She might be unhappy, in general, that she woke up. If she truly wanted to end it, she'll be angry at whoever brought her here."

Sam waved a hand. "Lucky me. Whatever, she can be as pissed as she wants. I wasn't going to let her die."

"Tell her that," Evanston said. "Remind her that there are people who care about her very much. She'll have to undergo extensive therapy. You might find it beneficial to sit in on some of it."

"Maybe." Sam wasn't so sure. The only therapy sessions he'd seen had been on TV and in movies, and they'd been grueling. He didn't know if he was strong enough for that kind of introspection. "That stuff is pretty intense."

"Mel's going to have to do the work," Travis said. "The choice of whether she makes a turnaround or not has got to be hers."

Sam sighed thoughtfully. "I'll be there every step of the way," he decided at that moment. "We'll do the work together."

A crease furrowed Travis' brow, and he looked away.

Evanston moved toward the door. "I'll be back later to check on her. The nurses have instructions to call me if she wakes up."

Sam looked at Mel. "When."

The doctor said, "Excuse me?"

He gazed at Evanston. "*When* she wakes up."

Smiling, the doctor conceded. "*When* she wakes up. Of course." He turned to Travis. "She may just make it yet, if she's half as tenacious as her brother. He seems like a good man to have in her corner."

"He is a good man," Travis agreed, and went to stare out of the window facing the nurses' station.

The doctor left and Sam turned back to Mel.

"Saint Samuel," Travis muttered.

Sam bristled at the tone and cocked his head. "What was that?"

Travis faced him. "All of a sudden, I'm seeing things in our future that I'd never envisioned in a million years. Rehab, therapy sessions, twelve step programs… That's what you being there 'every step of the way' sounds like to me."

"Maybe it does. What did you think I was going to do? Say, 'You tried to kill yourself, Mel, so to hell with you, you're on your own now'?"

"Of course not. But there are inpatient facilities that could guide her through the process she needs. Why does the only person who can help her have to be you?"

"Because she's part of me, Travis, and if you don't get that by now then you really don't know me at all. I'll never abandon my twin sister to some cold facility."

Travis' face reddened. "I never said you should abandon her. I'm just not sure you should place her as high on your list of priorities as you do. She certainly doesn't hold you in the same esteem."

"You're basing this diagnosis on what, Doctor? The handful of times you've seen her over the past few months?"

"Sam, listen. You're bending over backwards for someone who hasn't shown you the same consideration for months now. I'm just saying, I don't see why you have to put your life on hold to take care of her above all else."

Sam chuckled bitterly. "Are you fucking kidding me? My life has been on hold since the day I met you. I told you before and it's still true today—we don't know what we have, or don't have, until Mel gets her act together and we figure out where all the pieces fit into the puzzle. Nothing has changed, Trav. There are just a few more pieces to make fit, now."

Travis clenched his fists open and closed at his sides. He finally said, "I guess I never told you... I can put up with a lot, but I really hate puzzles."

Sam felt as if he were falling. He clutched the handrail on the bed to keep from stumbling, even though he was standing still. He'd never seen such a cold, unfriendly expression on Travis' face. It scared him worse than anything he could recall of late. He inhaled and blew out the breath, hoping his voice didn't squeak when he finally used it. "I guess it's good we found this out now."

Travis' chuckle held no humor. "Now *you're* fucking kidding *me*. I don't see anything good in this situation at all." He glanced around the room. "I've got to get out of here."

"Fine. Go home, go to work, I don't care. Just go, Travis. I need to be with my sister. I definitely don't need this."

His parting look was full of hurt and anger. "You don't have the slightest concept of what you need, Sam Madison. You have no fucking idea." Travis walked out and thudded the sliding door closed behind him.

Sam dropped into the nearest chair, still clutching the handrail. He rested his face against the cool metal and hoped that when he opened his eyes, Travis would still be sleeping across Mel's feet. *Maybe it was all just a dream. Scratch that, a nightmare.*

He opened his eyes, and Mel was staring at him.

Sam's eyes bugged out and he sprang forward. "Mel! You're awake!"

"Where am I?" Her voice was hoarse.

"Cook County Hospital. They think you tried to kill yourself."

"If this isn't Heaven, then I didn't do a very good job of it." She glanced around. "But then again, you did say Cook County. So maybe I'm in Hell."

He clasped her hand. "Why, Mel? I know things have been rough lately, but I guess I thought they were getting better. Of course you miss Rob, but you had Ronna and Derek—"

"Ronna is gone. She took Pete and went home to her parents until her husband comes back. And Derek, well, Derek is a grade 'A' asshole. I thought he was interested in me as a person, but it turns out he really just wanted to use me as a drug runner." Her voice became stronger the more she talked. "I found out last night when he took me to some guy's house and made me go inside to deliver some shit. Let's just say the guy and his friend wanted more than the drugs I had to deliver. I called Derek real quick, because he was waiting for me out in the car. Do you know what he told me?"

Sam shook his head, almost afraid to hear.

She scoffed. "He told me to do whatever they wanted, and he'd wait. It was all part of the deal, he told me. So... I did it. The two of them—"

"Raped you?" Sam's gut churned.

Mel chuckled sadly. "You can't call it rape when you go along willingly, Sammy. They gave me some cocaine and at some point they injected something into my arm, too. I was pretty out of it. The whole scene was one frigging long orgasm until they decided they were done with me. They poured me back into most of my clothes and dropped me off at Derek's car. When they paid him they said something about his 'whore', and tossed a few more bills my way. Derek just laughed. He drove me home and stuck me in bed, then left again."

Sam thought he might be sick. He rose and paced around the room.

"The drugs started wearing off, I guess. I thought about everything they'd done, and I didn't know if they'd used condoms or not. I tried to clean myself up, but I was just too tired. I wanted to sleep, but I couldn't come down. And eventually, I just wanted it to be over. I found those pills I had left over from the accident, and took a bunch of them."

He looked at her. "So it wasn't a premeditated, planned thing. You didn't really want to commit suicide, you were just reacting to the rape. That makes a difference on how the doctors look at it, Mel."

She gazed at him levelly. "Of course I tried to kill myself, because it wasn't a rape. I didn't want to face the consequences of what I'd become. A whore."

"You're not a whore!" he snapped. "You were drugged and taken advantage of. The doctors did a rape kit. They can turn it over to the cops and you can press charges against Derek and the other scumbags who did this to you."

"Oh yeah, so they can tell the police I was there delivering drugs? Pull your head out, Sammy. No one is going to tell the cops anything. I may be crazy, but I'm sane enough to want to stay out of jail."

Sam's mind raced. "Okay, we won't say anything. But the doctor is going to ask if you were raped, so you'd better have a plausible answer."

She smiled. "Not rape. Just one hell of a gang bang."

He slapped the back of the chair he'd been sitting in. "Damn it, Mel! This isn't a joke. Levi and I found you yesterday. We thought you were dead. It was really brutal and awful."

"Yesterday? Wow. I lost a day somewhere. Must have been some good shit."

He found himself clenching and unclenching his fists, much the same as Travis had done earlier. "Nothing about this is good, Mel. You've caused a lot of pain to the people who love you the most, do you get that?"

She shrugged. "Sorry, Sammy. What else can I say?"

It pained him to admit it, but the path was becoming clearer. "You can tell them that yes, you did try to kill yourself."

"Okay." Mel shrugged again.

Sam gathered all the strength he could muster and headed to the door. "They asked me to let them know when you woke up. I'll send the nurse in now."

"Tell her I need something for my headache. Oxy, maybe? And something to drink. My throat is parched."

He kept walking but waved a hand. At the nurses' station he stopped to speak to the woman who'd been taking care of Mel. "My sister is awake. She doesn't seem to be suffering from a loss of memory. She says she wasn't raped, but instead had drugged-up, consensual sex two nights ago."

"Okay." The woman gazed at him uncomfortably.

Sam kept talking. "Melanie admitted that she wanted to kill herself. She's also drug seeking, asking for more oxycodone. I'd like her placed on a three-day psych hold." He walked past the nurse and out of the door.

* * * *

Travis drove home and walked straight through the house to the bedroom. He'd already let his office know he wouldn't be coming in, and was seriously considering taking a long bike ride to burn off some steam. He'd have time after that to catch a nap and then he could pick Levi up from day camp. Just to be safe, he'd wait to call his mom until he was sure he could make the pick-up.

"Yeah, that's what I'll do." He stretched out on the bed. "A nice long ride is just what I need. I could do the thirty mile route, or maybe fifty if I don't want as long of a nap." He closed his eyes.

When he opened them again, he heard noises coming from the kitchen. Yawning, he strolled out there and was surprised to see his mom, Sam and Levi baking cookies. "Whoa." Travis glanced at the clock. *Four p.m.* "What the hey? I just closed my eyes for a minute."

"Yeah!" Levi laughed and Kim chuckled.

"We've been here almost two hours, son. You were snoring when we arrived."

Travis made a face. "I *don't* snore."

They all looked at Sam, who only made eye contact with Levi. "Maybe just a little."

Levi hooted again and handed a cookie to Travis. "Chocolate chip. We're going to take some to Mommy in the hospital."

He accepted the cookie and looked at Sam. "I'm surprised to see you here. Is she awake?"

Sam wiped off the counter. "Yeah, she woke up this morning. Doesn't seem to have any memory loss or other issues. But she will need to stay there for at least three days."

Levi added, "Uncle Sammy said I can't go see her, but he can take the cookies. And we're taking some home to Grandpa Dave."

Travis exchanged glances with his mom. "Grandpa Dave?" he mouthed.

She smiled and shrugged. "Try your cookie. We think they're pretty darn good."

He ate it and nodded. "Really good. Do we have any milk?"

"It would probably be in the fridge," Sam commented, and washed his hands in the sink. "Okay, you two," he said to Levi and Kim. "I'm going to grab a quick shower and a nap. Don't wait dinner on me, I'm beat. I might sleep through 'til morning."

"Have a good rest." Kim patted his cheek.

Levi stood on tiptoes to pat the other side. "Sweet dreams, Uncle Sammy."

He rubbed noses with the boy. "Right back atcha, kiddo. If I don't see you later I'll see you tomorrow for sure." He strolled down the hall.

Travis looked at his mom again. "Excuse me just a minute."

She reached for his biceps and squeezed. "He's tired, Trav. Why don't you give him some space?"

"I will. Be right back." He followed Sam down the hall and closed the bedroom door behind him.

Sam had already started the shower running and was peeling off his clothes.

"Want some company?" Travis teased.

Sam still wouldn't look him in the eye. "I'm beat, man. I just want to smell decent and sleep."

"You smell decent to me."

"Yeah, well, we both know you're weird, so..." He entered the shower and closed the door.

"I could wash your back," Travis called over the spray.

"Rain check," Sam replied.

He walked out of the bathroom and back down the hall. His mom and Levi had just finished cleaning the kitchen.

"Dad's grilling halibut for dinner, with steamed vegetables. Would you like to join us?" she asked him.

"Aw, sounds good, but I don't think so, Mom." He glanced at Levi. "Are you joining them?"

"Yeah! Grandpa Dave said maybe we can go fishing sometime, and then we can cook what we catch."

"Well, okay then. And how's camp? Are you having fun?"

He nodded enthusiastically. "I passed another level in swimming lessons. I floated. Jimmy didn't pass yet. He sank."

Travis chuckled. "Poor Jimmy. I hope someone rescued him."

"The teacher did. Jimmy's my best camp friend. Grandma said maybe he can spend the night sometime. She'll have to talk to Jimmy's mom first, though."

"I see. And are you enjoying sleeping in my old room?"

"Yes! Grandma showed me the marks on the wall to show how tall you were. We're the same size at age six."

"We are? Cool. Sounds like things are going okay, then. Mom, would you mind if he spent another night? I think Sam really needs some peace and quiet to rest."

"I figured we'd keep him. You just let me know when you're ready for him to come home." She packed up cookies to take and left some for them, and a plate for Mel.

Travis walked them out and gave both of them hugs before they drove off. When he returned to the house he locked everything up and sauntered back to the bedroom.

Sam was lying in bed. He closed his eyes quickly when Travis walked in.

"I know you're not asleep. I also know you're mad at me, and I don't blame you. I said some shitty things this morning, Sam. I was tired and grouchy and I shouldn't have said them."

Sam opened his eyes. "So you're not saying you didn't mean them, or that you're sorry. You're just saying that you shouldn't have said them."

Travis smiled sheepishly. "Pretty much."

"Asshole." He rolled over, away from Travis.

Rather than force the issue, Travis decided to take a quick shower and see how Sam felt after he'd gotten some much needed sleep. He cleaned up and brushed his teeth, then slipped between the covers.

Sam's breathing was steady and even.

Travis couldn't resist reaching out and running a hand down his back.

Sam didn't flinch.

Leaning in, he pressed light kisses to the back of Sam's shoulder blade.

Still no movement, except for Travis' cock, which had hardened once he'd climbed in bed with his lover. He knew he should leave Sam alone and let him sleep. He just couldn't seem to help himself.

Travis pressed his naked body against Sam's, nude except for boxers. He reached a hand inside Sam's underwear and fondled his cock until it slowly came to life. He kissed the warm back and shoulder again, and nuzzled everywhere he could reach.

His own cock throbbed painfully, in need of sweet relief. He wedged it between Sam's ass cheeks and rubbed.

"Wha—?" Sam mumbled, suddenly awake.

"Shhh," Travis whispered. "Stay calm and let me love you."

"No!" Sam pushed him away. "This is *not* okay, after what you said to me today."

"The truth hurts, babe, I get that. I know we've got some talking to do about Mel, and what's going to happen, but there's time for that later. We need *this* now to remind us of what's really important." He grabbed Sam's arm.

Sam shoved away again. "Mel is important to me. That's *my* truth. Don't patronize me and act like my thoughts and feelings are cute, but they aren't the *right* thoughts and feelings. You've been doing it for months now, and I've had enough of it. If we're ever going to be anything to each other it's equal partners, and both of our feelings count."

"Of course they do." Travis knew his voice *was* patronizing, and it was obvious he was just trying to placate Sam so they could have sex. He couldn't reel himself in. He reached for Sam's arm again.

Sam slapped his hand away.

Travis slapped Sam's hand back.

They stared at each other, both breathing hard.

Sam slapped Travis across the face.

Travis smacked him right back.

They wrestled on the bed for a moment, first Sam was on top then they flipped and Travis was. Gripping each other's biceps, they rolled and fell out of bed, scratching and clawing at each other.

"Fuck you!" Sam shouted.

"That's what I was trying to do!" Travis yelled back.

"You're a cocky, self-centered bastard and I wouldn't fuck you if you had the last cock on Earth."

"Well you're an immature, insecure masochist who thinks letting your sister trample all over you is the only way you can help her. And if I did have the last cock on Earth, I'd stick it inside you right now because

I'm so turned on I'm going to explode if I can't have you."

Panting, Sam stared at him for a moment before grabbing his face and kissing him hard. The pressure caused friction, adding to the sting of the slap.

Travis groaned.

His lover spread his legs and spit in his hand, then reached down and wet his own hole. He spit again and slicked it over Travis' throbbing shaft. Sam put his face an inch away from Travis' and murmured, "Fuck me, then. And if you ever hit me again, I'll be out of here so fast, the only thing you'll feel is my breeze."

Travis nudged his cockhead to Sam's hole. "Same goes, you irritating prick. You need to learn how to act when someone's trying to help you."

Sam bucked his hips as the crown slipped in. "Why do you always think I need your help? Maybe I just want to *be* with you, without feeling like you're constantly trying to take care of me."

He pushed his shaft forward and the tight sphincter sucked him in. Travis took a moment to savor the heat, then looked at Sam again. "And why are you and I so fucking much alike? You're constantly trying to help Mel. You don't think she gets just as sick of that?"

Sam bit his lip as the pummeling began. "Well, fuck, yeah! She probably does. And that's another thing. Why the fuck are you always right?"

Travis drove deep and wrapped his arms around Sam's warm body. He nuzzled his man's neck and whispered, "Because I know you, you crazy bastard. I know what you and I need. And I love you more than I've ever loved anyone in this life. When I heard you talking to Mel last night about her completing you, and being the other half of your heart, I wanted to die because that's how I feel about you, you stupid fuck."

"Aw, God." Sam shuddered and his eyes rolled back in his head. "Jack me and make me come."

Travis squeezed the leaking cock that waved between them and tugged the shaft. A few good pulls and Sam erupted, spraying cum in the air, covering both of them. He jerked his lover off until he was spent, then drew him close. "Now kiss me, and make me come."

Sam obliged, his tongue taking control of Travis' mouth.

Travis pumped a few more times into the hot and waiting ass, then he blew. His seed erupted into Sam's channel and it felt so good, he wished he could crawl in there after it. He thrust as deep as he could, over and over, until he couldn't any longer.

Sam cupped his face and they kissed, and kissed some more.

Travis thought if he stayed in there long enough his cock would firm up again, and they could just keep going, but his shaft slipped out. He curled up in Sam's arms and they lay on the floor, each breathing heavily.

"Aw God, Sam. I'm sorry. I'm so sorry for everything. Please tell me we're okay. I was panicking after I left the hospital this morning. I almost came back and apologized then."

"I panicked, too, but then Mel woke up. She told me what happened the night she OD'd, how Derek sent her to deliver drugs to two guys who wanted more than just crack from her. And when she went to Derek for help, he told her to give them whatever they wanted."

Travis groaned. "Aw, fuck. She was raped."

"No, she swears it was consensual. They drugged her up and fucked her sideways, then tossed her in Derek's car and threw money at her. She was sick by the time she got home, and that's when she swallowed the pills."

"The hospital has the rape kit. She can press charges."

"She was delivering drugs to them. She enjoyed the sex, until she didn't anymore. Mel doesn't want to get in trouble and risk jail time. The shitty part is, she doesn't know if they used condoms. She could have an STD, or worse."

"Damn, Sam."

"Yeah. Then she asked me to get her more oxy. That's when I told the nurse to put her on the three-day psych hold."

Travis squeezed one of Sam's hands. "I think that was the right move."

"I do too. I'm not sure what the *next* right move will be, but I guess I have two more days to figure that out."

"I'm here if you need help with that."

Sam smiled. "Of course I do. And yeah, we're okay. I love you, Trav. I need you."

"I need you too, babe. More than anything." Travis pulled him close and they shared a sweet and salty kiss.

Chapter Ten

Sam went to visit Mel on the last day of her required hold. He hadn't stayed long each of the previous days, and figured the final day wouldn't be much better. She was off all meds and feeling it, and cranky as hell without cigarettes.

He'd taken her something from Levi each day, but hadn't told anyone that she'd thrown the chocolate chip cookies across the room and they'd ended up in the trash. The second day she'd been a little smarter with the banana nut bread. He figured the brownies would be a hit as well.

"Hey," he said as the nurse allowed him into her room.

Mel gazed at him dully. "So what's the word? Do I get to go home today?"

"Levi made you some brownies." He held them out but didn't automatically hand them over, remembering the cookies.

"Thanks." She accepted them and opened the plastic wrap to nibble them. "Who's helping him do all this baking? Last time I checked, you didn't know how to turn an oven on."

He sat in the chair next to her bed. "I do too. But it's Travis' mom. They're having fun spending some time together after day camp gets out."

"Doesn't she work?"

"She and her husband are both high-school teachers. They're out for the summer."

Mel nodded. "That'd be a nice job."

Sam leaned back in his chair. "What about you, Mel? Any ideas on what might be a good job for you?"

She broke off another piece of brownie and popped it in her mouth. "I could be an official brownie taste-tester. These are pretty awesome."

He smiled. "Let me know if you find someone willing to pay you for that. I might sign up, too."

She set the plate on her tray table and crossed her arms. "I don't know. Obviously I can't go back to the bar."

"Not sure why you'd want to."

"All my friends are there."

"Derek is there."

She shrugged and picked at one of her fingernails. "Being with him was better than being alone."

Sam sighed. "You're not going to be alone. We'll figure out the living arrangements, but first you've got to make sure you're clean. The doctor here gave me the name of a good rehab center that accepts the state-funded medical insurance you just got. Travis made some calls. It sounds like a good place."

"Travis," she muttered. "He's such an uptight asshole. What do you see in him, Sammy?"

"He's really not, Mel. You don't know him, and he doesn't know you, either. I'd like to change that once you're feeling better."

"If he's still around. You may have moved on by then."

He gazed at her levelly. "He'll be around. We love each other, Mel. We've talked about the future, and what we both want. It's a little up in the air right now, but that's okay. We have time."

She frowned. "You're waiting for me to get better so I can take Levi back? Sorry, I'm not sure when that's gonna happen."

"That's not it at all. We love Levi, sis. We enjoying spending time with him. He's becoming part of our family."

Her eyes narrowed. "What are you saying, exactly?"

Sam shifted uncomfortably. He hadn't intended to broach this subject yet, not alone, and not when Mel was still so fragile. He tested the waters carefully. "We wouldn't mind if Levi stayed with us." *Permanently*, he added in his brain. *We wouldn't mind if Levi stayed with us permanently.* He just couldn't say the word. Mel was calm right now. He suspected she might not be if he told her the rest of his thoughts.

"Oh, good. So I have more time to get my shit together, then. That's great. I can use it. I'm glad he's behaving, and not too much trouble." She offered Sam the first smile he'd seen in a long time. "You know, I really appreciate your taking care of him. I've never told you that, and so I figured it was time."

"I love Levi. I'll always be here for him," Sam said truthfully. He wanted to add, *Travis feels the same way.* He just couldn't do it. Instead, he changed the subject. "So you think the rehab facility might be okay? I believe things will be a lot easier for you once you're off the drugs and cigarettes."

She blinked. "Cigarettes too? Why? They aren't illegal."

He shot her a look. "They're over five bucks a pack, Mel. You can't afford them. Besides, they're bad for your health and while you're tackling addictions, you might as well tackle that one."

"I'm really not addicted," she complained.

"And I'm really not gay. I just like sleeping with guys."

"What a coincidence! Me too! You probably like them one at a time, though."

"Generally speaking, yeah."

She frowned. "Me too. Damn, that Derek was an asshole."

"Forget about Derek. He's history."

"I should still have a paycheck coming from the bar. I don't know what's going to happen to all my stuff, either, if he's still at the apartment."

"We'll take care of it. Travis talked about renting a storage unit for your things until you're ready for them again."

"I could just go back to the apartment, as long as Derek was gone."

Sam shook his head. "You're not going back there again. Your next place is going to be clean and bug-free. I plan to make sure of that."

"And big enough for Levi to have room to play, something with a yard would be nice. If I can afford it."

He bit his lip. *Maybe if Mel saw Levi at Travis' house, she'd realize how happy he is there. Maybe...later.* "Which brings us back around to the job. What would you *like* to do, Mel?"

She shrugged. "I like to draw."

"That's something. You're good at it, too. We'd just have to figure out a way to make money at it. Maybe you could go back to school to become a graphic artist, or something like that."

She ran her hands through her shaggy hair. "That's too much to think about now, Sammy. When I get overwhelmed I start to freak out."

"You're right, there's no need to worry about that now. The rehab program lasts at least a month, but it might be longer if they think—or you think—you need more time."

"Will you come visit me?"

"Absolutely. It's an hour drive, so I can't promise to come every day, but I'll do the best I can."

"Okay." Mel nodded. "I need to do something to turn this ship around. Might as well start with rehab."

Sam reached for her and drew her into a hug.

Mel clung to him tightly.

He felt her hot tears soak through the back of his shirt. "This is going to be good, Mel. I really think it's just what you need."

"I hope so, Sammy. God, I hope so."

* * * *

Sam and Travis dropped Levi off with Kim and Dave after dinner, then drove to the bar to see about Mel's final paycheck. Derek explained that he paid in cash, and gave Sam several hundred dollars. Sam wanted to tell the son of a bitch what he really thought about him, but knew nothing good could come of that. Derek had paid him without argument and said his things were all out of the apartment. They were done with him, and Sam left it at that. He and Travis agreed the extra cash was probably the owner's way of saying he was glad Mel hadn't raised a stink after the night she was brutally used.

At the apartment, he found that Derek had cleaned out almost everything of value except Mel's clothes.

Sam didn't really care. The furniture stayed with the apartment, and she could replace the dishes and things that Derek had taken. They wouldn't need a storage unit after all. They packed Mel's clothes and personal items and loaded them into the back of the Lexus and Mel's car. Sam left the keys with the Super, explaining that his sister was ill and unable to clean the place properly. Sam suggested they keep the security deposit for cleaning fees, and the Super was appeased.

"Aw, hell," Travis chuckled as they stood on the street by her car. "He won't use the money to have the place cleaned. He'll pocket the dough and sweep the place out, and call it good."

"No shit." Sam shuddered. "I'm happy to be rid of that apartment."

"Me too. Tonight we'll wash the clothes she'll need to take with her tomorrow, and the rest can wait until later. In the garage. Fucking cockroaches."

Sam nodded. "Thanks, babe. I appreciate your help."

"I'm actually surprised that it didn't take longer. Mom's planning on keeping Levi overnight. I figured we'd be packing late into the night."

"She didn't have that much stuff."

"Especially once Derek was done going through it."

"It's fine," Sam decided. "She's making a fresh start. We'll help her buy new stuff when she needs it."

"Agreed." He glanced at Sam. "So, we have the house to ourselves tonight."

"And about four loads of laundry to do."

Travis rolled his eyes. "It's not like we have to wash it by hand, beat it against a rock or something. We stick it in the washer and then we have an hour to do something else." He waggled his eyebrows.

Sam grinned. "Does this mean I get to kiss the cat?"

"Mmm-hmm. And I think the cat wants to be kissed leaning over the kitchen table. Or maybe tossed over the back of the sofa. Somewhere we can't do it with the pipsqueak in the house."

Sam smiled. "And to think, Mel asked me what I see in you. Of course, I couldn't tell her I'm really in love with the cat."

"Of course. What did you tell her? What *do* you see in me?"

"Somehow, I avoided the question. I never got the chance to tell her what a caring, supportive, thoughtful and intelligent man you are."

"Aw." Travis blushed.

"With the biggest, most gorgeous cock I've ever had the pleasure to swallow, and a tongue that would make any woman jealous."

His lover laughed. "Oh yeah, you should have told her that. Right."

"It's the truth."

"Then let's get home and get busy. Park the car on the street, will you?"

"I will." Sam gave him a quick kiss and got into Mel's car and started it up. He followed Travis home and parked, then walked into the garage.

Travis pushed the button and lowered the door behind them. "Let's hurry and sort her stuff out here. Two piles, wash tonight and wash later. You figure out that much, and I'll get the machine going." He climbed out of the car and looked at Sam over the hood. "Then I want you naked with a towel and some lube in the kitchen. My big fat cock is calling dibs on your sexy ass, for starters."

"I'm there." Sam winked and hurried to start sorting.

Twenty minutes later he was bent over and clutching the kitchen table, while Travis licked and sucked his ass in preparation for what was to come.

"Mmm," his lover nuzzled his crack. "I don't know why it feels so much more erotic *out* of the bedroom."

"Sex in the kitchen is naughty. What you're doing is naughty. Don't stop! I'm just sayin'…"

Chuckling, Travis spread his cheeks wider and drove his tongue deeper into Sam's musky hole.

Sam bucked his hips in approval. The table felt cool against his face, in contrast to the heat burning in his ass. He nearly blacked out whenever Travis went down on him this way, it felt so fucking good.

"Oh, yeah." Travis rose to reach for the bottle of lube. "I could eat your ass every night for dinner. Sweetest spot on your sexy body." He squirted the lube and let it drizzle over Sam's crack. "But right now, something else is hungry for that sweet spot." He nudged his cockhead to the opening and worked it around in the lube.

"Yes," Sam sighed. "I want that, too."

"Mmm, your ass is so receptive. It's already sucking the crown in."

Sam couldn't hold back his laugh. "Well, aren't you special? Even your cock wears a crown."

Travis chuckled. "You're gonna pay for that, you know it, right? Hang on, smartass. I'm gonna pummel you for insubordination to the king." He drove in with one stroke, not pausing like he usually did to allow Sam time to acclimate.

Sam groaned but didn't have any complaints. He'd discovered in their play that he liked it a bit rough on occasion, and Travis had just the right touch. "Yes," he hissed. "If I say something else inappropriate will you do that again?"

"Over and over, baby. You just say the word."

"Fuck me!" Sam ground out as Travis let him have it. He clutched the sides of the table and held on for dear life. The rough treatment had him so hot he was already itching to shoot his wad. "Damn, jack me, baby. I'm close."

"Music to my ears." Travis reached down and gripped Sam's shaft. "Let's have it, man. Fill my hand with your hot seed."

Sam groaned as he shattered and Travis pumped him to completion. When his lover released his cock, he brought the hand he'd used to his mouth and licked the spunk clean.

Travis leaned down to Sam and gave him a creamy kiss. Sam groaned again and Travis exploded.

Warm heat filled his ass, and once again Sam had to struggle to remain upright. He held tight until his man's load was spent, then raised his head for more musky kisses.

With a hand on the table on either side of him for purchase, Travis kissed him passionately. He eventually eased his cock out, and they faced each other to continue kissing and caressing.

"You're the best," Sam murmured affectionately.

"Only with you," Travis replied, eyes closed. "Only you, for the rest of my life."

"Only you," Sam agreed. "And the cat."

Travis' eyes popped open, and he smiled.

* * * *

Travis arrived home from work a few weeks later, and found Sam cooking dinner. "Hey, handsome. What's the occasion?" He kissed his fella and opened the oven door to check out what smelled so good.

"Pork chops," Sam offered. "No occasion. I just decided it's not fair to expect you to cook every night."

"I don't mind, you know I enjoy it. But you cooking for me is nice, too. Where's the boy?"

Sam checked the vegetables steaming on the stovetop. "Actually, Levi is spending the night at Jimmy's house. His mom will take them to camp in the morning, and I'll pick him up after."

"Okay. This is rather sudden, isn't it?"

"What's wrong? We've met Jimmy's parents and we like them. He's stayed here a couple of times. She thought it was their turn."

"I guess, but a little more notice might be nice. If we knew we were going to have a free night, we could have made some plans. We keep putting off going out with Colt Crawford and his partner because we always have Levi."

Sam leaned back against the counter. "I'm sorry. I didn't think you'd mind. You usually jump all over a free night. Which reminds me, we still need to buy more upholstery cleaner for the sofa." He grinned.

"I'm not against it, but it just feels sudden is all. I'm going to go change. I'll be right back."

"We'll be ready to eat when you're done," Sam called after him.

Travis changed from his work clothes into shorts and a tank top. He washed up and returned to the kitchen where Sam was setting the table.

They sat down and Sam admitted, "There is something I wanted to talk with you about. This is as good a time as any, with Levi gone."

An uneasy feeling settled in the pit of Travis' stomach. "I knew it. What's up, Sam?"

Sam forked a pork chop onto Travis' plate. "Nothing is *up*. We just need to talk about Mel. She's doing really well in rehab. The director says she could be released as early as next week."

"Is he sure? Thirty days isn't much in the grand scheme of things. I'd hate to see her relapse."

"I don't think she will. She's been talking about what comes next. We've even started looking at ads for apartments."

Travis chewed the bite in his mouth then pushed his plate away. His appetite was suddenly gone. "She wants Levi, doesn't she?"

"She never said it in those words. It's more like she *expects* Levi to come live with her. Because we've never suggested that he might not."

"Then I think it's high time we make that suggestion! We probably should have done it before now, Sam. She needs to know how we feel about him."

"There's something else. She seems to think that I'll be moving in with them, too. She's talking about a three bedroom place."

Travis blinked. "Did you set her straight? That scenario is not going to happen?"

He shook his head. "No, because that seems like the best answer to her. I didn't know what to say, how to tell her."

"You tell her that we love each other and your living here is permanent. You're not going anywhere. Jesus, Sam, I thought we were past this."

"Take it easy. I'm walking a fine line between you and her and I'm trying not to upset anyone."

"Especially her, because you don't really have a problem upsetting me."

"For Christ's sake, Travis, she's in *rehab*. Of course I'm being delicate with her. I'd never do anything to set her back."

Travis pressed his palms down on the table and tried to remain calm. He needed to collect his thoughts and be as precise and tactful as possible. "Okay, so here's what we need to do. We'll go talk to her together. Explain our situation, and that we'd like her to consider leaving Levi with us. A one bedroom apartment would be easier to find, anyway, and cheaper. She doesn't even have a job yet, does she?"

"No. She's been discussing it with her counselor, but so far nothing has jumped out at her."

"Jobs just don't 'jump out' at people, Sam. You have to work hard and go after the one you want. She's not ready yet, I can feel it."

"Now you're being mean because you want her to stay in rehab so we don't have to deal with this. Guess what, lover, it's time to deal. Without yelling, without hitting, hopefully without fighting, we need to figure this out."

Travis stood and paced. "I suppose she can come here, as long as she stays clean and doesn't smoke. I told you before, I won't be happy if she backtracks, or lies to us."

Sam stood and folded his arms across his chest. "And I told you before, this isn't a dictatorship, even if you do own the fucking house. If it's going to work, it's got to be an equal partnership. Mel is my twin sister and I won't have you coming down like a warden on her. That just isn't going to happen."

"Oh for fuck's sake, I know she's your twin sister. You throw it in my face every time we try to have a conversation about her. She's the most important person in your life. I got it, Sam. If I want a spot, I'm hereby put on notice that I'll be playing second fiddle to Melanie Madison for the rest of my life."

"Mel was right. You are an asshole. Most days I don't see it, and then something happens to remind me. Well here's another notice for you, Dr. Nelson. As soon as I can find an apartment, Levi and I will be moving in with Mel. If you can manage an attitude adjustment, I might keep you around as a fuck buddy. But if you keep disparaging my sister, I'll kick you to the curb and fuck my hand every damn night." Sam turned and walked down the hall.

Travis stared after him, slack jawed.

Sam paused and looked back. "I'll sleep in Levi's bed tonight. Don't come sniffing around for sex. It'll make you look more pathetic than you already do." He kept walking.

Travis dropped into a chair. Stunned beyond belief, he didn't know what to do or say next. So he walked to the garage, laced up a set of sneakers, and grabbed his helmet. He took off on his bike, trying to pedal away his demons.

He returned an hour later, sweaty and too tired to fight anymore. Walking through the kitchen, he saw that Sam had cleaned up and retreated to Levi's room again. He debated knocking on the door but wasn't exactly sure what he'd say. Fearing it would cause another argument, he went to his room and closed the door.

Travis showered and climbed into bed naked. He prayed that at some point in the night Sam would slip in and join him under the covers, but it never happened. He rose and dressed for work as usual, without ever seeing Sam.

He worked a morning shift in the clinic then rearranged his schedule and took the afternoon off. During the hour-long trip to the rehab center, he wondered if he'd run into Sam there, but realized that he'd be arriving just as Sam needed to pick Levi up from camp. He should be safe.

The woman behind the desk at the center asked Travis who he was, and he informed her he was Melanie Madison's brother-in-law. She made a call, then directed him back to the room Mel was staying in.

He knocked on the door.

"Come in," she called.

Travis opened the door and took a few steps inside.

"Travis! Is something wrong?"

"No. Well, yes. I mean, Levi's fine."

She sat in one of two overstuffed chairs, and motioned for him to take the other.

She looked much better than the previous times he'd seen her. Her hair was clean and pulled back, and her eyes were clear. He sat and stared at her, unsure where to begin. "I need your help," he finally said.

"What is it?"

"It's…Sam. We fought last night. I don't know if he's been here to talk to you today, or not."

"No, he hasn't. What was the fight about?"

He gazed at her sheepishly. "You."

Mel chuckled. "Geez. Sorry. I didn't know. My ears weren't burning or anything."

Travis shook his head. "I don't mean to put this on you. It's not your fault, it's just something that happened."

"Let me guess. My brother wants me to come and live in your house and you're against it."

"No, actually that was my suggestion. He wants to get an apartment for you and Levi and him."

Her eyes widened. "Why would he want that? Last I heard he was madly in love with you."

Travis smiled. "Apparently, I can be a real asshole."

She shrugged. "I didn't think you could ever have too many assholes between gay men."

He laughed outright. "Good one. Sam told me I'd like you if I ever got to know you."

"Yeah, I heard the same muckety-muck. Seriously, Travis, what is he thinking?"

Travis inhaled and blew the breath out. *Time for full disclosure.* "He's afraid to upset you. He doesn't think he can be open and honest with you since you're in rehab."

"Well that's ridiculous. My counselor and I have spent many sessions discussing my being honest with people. I think I've done really well with it. I told Sam that I'm not ready to live on my own, or even with my family. I'm feeling pretty strong in here, but let's face it, this is a safe place. There aren't any temptations for me to deal with. I'd like to think if someone offered me a cigarette or a bong right now I'd be strong enough to say 'no'. But I'm not quite there yet."

He was surprised. "Sam didn't tell me. He acted like you guys were here looking at want ads for apartments together."

She waved a hand. "Oh, we were, but it was just looking. I know where I'll be going. There's a halfway house for people like me not far from here. We live together so we can support each other, and it's close so we can come to daily group meetings. They're like AA, but they're here, with people we know. They tell me people usually stay in the halfway houses for six months to a year, depending on the person. I think that sounds like just what I need. I've even been there, and it's a neat and clean place. No bugs." She smiled.

Travis held his breath. "What about Levi?"

She scratched her chin. "I agree, Levi is a problem. I can't take him to the halfway house. Kids aren't allowed, but it wouldn't be fair to him, anyway. I was trying to work up the courage to ask Sam if you guys could keep him a while longer."

He slowly shook his head. "I don't think so, Mel."

She blinked.

He leaned in and took her hand. "You see, Levi isn't a problem to us. We love him like he's our own. We *want* him to be our own. By all accounts he's happier than he's ever been, living with us. He loves my parents to pieces and they dote on him like they would a grandchild. But it's not fair to him, or us, to keep dangling this arrangement as temporary. The boy needs stability. If he's living with us he'll be in a different school this fall. We can't just bounce him back and forth between us on a whim."

She gripped Travis' hand. "I know. I've seen the change in him myself. On one hand it kills me, but on the other it thrills me. He's happy! My boy is so frigging happy. I'm not sure I could get him back now if I tried. But the idea of not being his mother anymore—"

"You will *always* be his mother. You see, that's one of the perks of giving him to two gay dads. You still get to be the mom." Travis smiled. "Sam and I want to get married and adopt Levi. As long as you stay clean, you can be in his life as much as you want. I'll be blunt with you here, Mel, that this is what pissed Sam off. If you don't stay clean, I couldn't let you be around Levi. You get that, don't you?"

"Absolutely." Tears streamed down her face. "I couldn't see it when I was strung out, but now it's as plain as daylight. I wouldn't want a druggie around my kid, either. Would you agree to make that part of the legal arrangements? As long as I'm clean and sober, I'll be allowed to have contact with him?"

"Absolutely," Travis repeated and squeezed her hand again. He reached in his pocket and removed a handkerchief. He started to hand it to her but reconsidered, and wiped her face himself.

She let him. "Travis, in case you haven't figured it out, Sam is very protective of me. It's been me and him against the world for a lot of years. We didn't have the best childhood."

"I heard about some of it."

"And when I met Rob, Sam didn't like him one bit. Rob was a homophobic jerk, but I put up with it because he was my jerk, and I loved him. And for all his jerkiness, he loved me and Levi. When he went away I lost it, and that's when things started spiraling downward."

"I'm sorry, Mel."

"Sam always wanted to fix things, but he just couldn't chase away the demons. I had to do that myself. I feel like I'm suddenly, yet slowly, doing it right this time. It feels good."

He smiled. "I've been accused of trying to fix things for Sam. Maybe it would feel good to him if I let him do it himself, too."

"I think you're right."

Travis glanced at the table next to her chair and spotted a drawing pad with sketches on it. "What's that?"

She followed his gaze. "Oh, my drawings." She picked them up and held the pad out to him.

He flipped through the pages and paused when he saw the most beautiful sketch of Levi's face. "Oh, wow. Did you do this from a picture?"

"No. From a memory in my head."

He gazed at her. "These are really good, Mel."

She grinned. "Yeah. Sam and I were trying to figure out a job where I could make money doing what I loved. I mean, prostitution is illegal, so something *else* that I love. He didn't think brownie taste-tester would pay very well, either."

Travis laughed. "I might have an idea. Did you know tattoo artists use sketches like these for their art all the time? Some of them are good at drawing like you are, but some rely on artwork from other sources. I know a guy you should talk to."

Mel chuckled. "How do you know a guy like that, Reverend Trav? Sam told me you were really pissed when he mentioned wanting a tat."

"Sam is so full of shit." He stood and began unbuttoning his shirt.

She looked surprised, and they locked gazes.

He pulled his shirt off and his inked skin came into view.

"Oh my God! Look at all those tattoos. You're a marked man."

He turned around so she could see his back was just as covered. Facing her again, he said, "The rest of me is inked as well."

"I want to see," she said breathily.

"I'm afraid you'd have to buy me dinner first."

Mel laughed and stood. "Can I touch you?"

"Waist up, no problem."

She ran her hands along his chest and arms, then turned him around and did the same to his back. "God, Trav," she whispered. "If I had a dick it'd be hard right now."

He smiled over his shoulder at her. "You're a lot like your brother. But I'm definitely a gay man."

Mel leaned in and whispered, "You make *me* want to be a gay man, too. But I'll control myself because I love my brother and I'm happy as hell for him. Now, put your shirt back on and let's figure out how to bring Sammy around to our way of thinking." She patted his ass for good measure.

Travis gaped at her.

Mel winked.

Chapter Eleven

Sam glanced at his reflection in the mirror and studied his first tattoo ever. The back of his right shoulder now sported the spitting image of Levi, courtesy of a sketch done by Mel and the tattooing skills of Eddie Ortega. "It's gorgeous. I fucking love it."

Travis gazed at the tattoo, his face an expression of awe. "Holy crap. Seeing you with a tat makes me want to jump you right here and now, man."

Eddie brushed a strand of long gray hair off his face. "I really wish you wouldn't. I'm a tolerant guy and all for free love, but some things I don't need to see firsthand."

"Yeah, me either." Mel feigned an eye roll. She turned to Eddie. "Watching you was amazing. I was loaded when I got my tat, and don't remember a thing about it."

"Stupid and illegal," he spouted, and glanced at her arm. "And don't call that toad on your arm a tat. If I were you, I'd choose one of those nice drawings you've done, and have me ink you a cover up. It'll be big, but between your artwork and mine it could be spectacular."

She grinned. "I might just do that."

Sam watched the exchange. Eddie was an old friend of Travis' but the guy was definitely eccentric. Sixty if he was a day, he had a long gray braid running down his back and a full, bushy beard. His T-shirt advertised 'Free Mustache Rides' so he was obviously a ladies' man. Sam wasn't sure he liked the looks Eddie tossed in Mel's direction.

She smiled at the old fart again. "So, do you think you could use some of these drawings?"

"I know I could. Give me your phone number and the next time I get a special request I'll call you. I usually take a couple of days to work up an image, so that should give you enough time, too."

"Great!" She beamed.

Sam thought she looked five years younger without the drug pall over her. He was thrilled that she seemed to be thriving.

Mel walked around the tattoo shop, looking at all the patterns and designs on the walls. She nosed behind the counter and commented, "This place could use some organization."

"We get along just fine," Eddie replied.

"A woman's touch, you know." She batted her eyelashes.

He gazed at her levelly, his eye wrinkles betraying every one of his years. "I couldn't pay you big bucks."

"I wouldn't need big bucks, just enough to get by. I think I could learn so much from you. I might even want to try tattooing."

He made a thoughtful face and nodded. "Can you learn piercing? That would be helpful. Piercing is a pain in my ass, so to speak."

"Of course!" She clapped her hands together. "I'd love that."

"We might just be able to work something out." He put a plastic bandage over Sam's tattoo and gave him care instructions. "If you forget something, ask him." He jerked his thumb toward Travis. "One hundred and twelve tattoos later, he ought to know the drill."

Travis smiled. "I've got my eye on one-thirteen. I really love that picture of Levi. It makes a great chattoo." He looked at Eddie. "Levi's terminology."

Eddie blinked. "Where are we going to put the kid? On your ass?"

"Maybe my hip?"

The tattoo artist nodded. "I could manage that." He looked at Sam. "I do asses, but that's not the best place for a picture of your kid. Unless he's a little shit." He laughed at his own joke. "And I won't do Mr. Winky. No needles should ever come near Mr. Winky."

Travis nodded in firm agreement.

"Um, right." Sam bit back a laugh. He paid then Eddie and Mel exchanged phone numbers. Travis gave Eddie a quick hug and they left with promises to be back soon.

"He's done all your ink?" Sam asked as Travis drove.

"All but the first two. He made some little changes to those later, though, so he could claim my whole body."

"Gee, and I thought I had claim to your whole body."

"Just the cat." Travis winked at him.

Sam smiled. They'd been okay since Mel had revealed her halfway house plan to him, and he'd been able to tell Travis he wasn't moving out. They'd argued a couple more times but Trav had been quick to apologize, and the makeup sex had been totally worth it. Things were good, on the surface at least. Down a little deeper, their lives were still on edge as he'd never gotten up the courage to ask Mel to consider giving them custody of Levi. Travis had been pissed, but had told him it was probably best not to talk about it. So they hadn't.

The next hurdle would come in a few weeks. They had to enroll Levi in school, but had yet to decide *which* school. Sam was a bundle of nerves when he let himself think about it.

Mel leaned forward. "Thanks for picking me up and dropping me off. I know it's a long way, but it was fun to watch my brother lose his tattoo cherry."

"It was fun." Travis grinned at her in the rear-view mirror. He glanced at Sam. "What do you think? Get another one some time, maybe?"

"Oh, hell yeah. Tomorrow, if we can find the right design. I might be addicted."

"I can suggest a group for that," Mel teased.

He turned sideways so he could look at her. "You look great, Mel. The halfway house is going okay then?"

"It's very good. I like the people there. We keep each other honest and real. And now, I have a job! I know it might not be very many hours at first, but if I hang around and make myself useful, pretty soon Eddie will be wondering what he did without me."

"That'll be great, Mel," Travis said.

"Watch yourself," Sam cautioned. "He looks like a dirty old man. What guy his age dresses like that?"

Travis chuckled. "Eddie is solid. Sure, he's a bit of an aging hippy, but I'd trust my life to him. In a way I have, on many occasions."

Sam nodded thoughtfully. Travis' endorsement made him feel a little better, but the guy had still made eyes at his sister. And she went gaga over his many tattoos, which were dozens more than most men his age probably had. *Perhaps it's best if I just don't think about it.*

Travis pulled up in front of the halfway house behind Mel's car. "It's twenty minutes from the shop to here. Can you manage a drive like that every day?"

She shrugged. "Twenty minutes isn't bad. Going anywhere outside your neighborhood in Chicago takes at least that long."

"True."

Sam glanced at the sidewalk and was surprised to see Kim, Dave and Levi standing there. "What's going on here?"

"You just stay put. I'll let you know when you can get out." Travis jumped from the car and Mel climbed out of the back.

"Where are you going?" Sam asked her.

"Do what you're told." She wagged a finger at him.

Sam made a questioning face at Kim.

She grinned and shrugged, but he could tell she was in on whatever Travis had up his sleeve.

He rolled down his window. "Hey, Levi! What's happening? What are you guys doing way out here?"

Before the boy could answer, Kim wrapped her hand over his mouth. With her other hand she waved a finger back and forth. "No, no, no. Wait and see."

Sam was intrigued.

When Travis came around and opened Sam's door, he'd donned a formal black bow tie over his shorts and T-shirt. "I was going to rent a tuxedo but it's too blinking hot out here. So picture me in a tux, okay?"

"Why not?" Sam grinned.

"And I could have chosen a fancier place to do this, but I wanted this particular group of people to be witnesses, and it was tough getting everyone together at a mutually convenient time and location. So this is what you get."

"O-kay." Sam shrugged.

Travis took Levi by the hand and walked him over to the Lexus, then lifted him up to Sam's lap. "Sam and Levi, you each know how much I love you. I've been talking with my parents, and they agree it's time to let the rest of the world know. Also, I've been talking with Mel, and we've reached an agreement that we'd like to make binding and legal." He pulled out a silver wedding band. "Sam, marry me, and make me the happiest man on the planet. I promise I'll never stop trying to make you the second happiest." He pulled a framed picture from behind his back and showed it to them. It was the drawing Mel had made of Levi, the basis for his tattoo. Under the image she'd written *Levi Madison-Nelson*. "Levi, Melanie will always be your mother. She'll always be here for you, and she'll never stop loving you. But she's agreed that we should make your living arrangements permanent. So once Sam and I are married we want to adopt you, and I'd like you to have both of our names. If *you'd* like that."

Sam was stunned. Travis slipped the band on his left ring finger and squeezed his hand, then studied Levi's reaction.

The boy glanced at each of their faces and ended up gazing at Mel. He jumped down and ran to her, giving her a big hug.

She leaned down to hold him tight.

"This is really okay?" he asked.

Through tears she nodded. "If it's what you want, baby. I just need you to be happy. I know those two daddies will make sure of that."

He glanced back at Sam and Travis. "I'll have *two* daddies?"

They both nodded.

A huge grin split his face. He looked back at Mel. "And you're still Mommy, right?"

"Always and forever. I love you, Levi. Your daddies and your grandparents love you, too. We'll be one big family."

He hugged her neck again.

"Are you happy, baby?"

Levi nodded enthusiastically. "If I was any happier, I might just float away." He grinned, then ran back to Travis and reached up to him.

Travis scooped him up.

"Daddy." Levi patted both of Travis' cheeks.

"Son." Travis nuzzled his neck. He leaned in toward Sam so Levi could pat his face the same way.

"Daddy."

Sam fought back tears. "Yes, son."

Travis pressed a kiss to Sam's temple. "You haven't accepted yet. I've got a bunch more promises for you, with regards to acceptable and unacceptable behavior. But I figured those are best discussed in private."

"I don't need any more promises. I love you, Trav. Yes, I'll marry you." They kissed, and Levi wrapped his arms around both of their necks, laughing. Sam inhaled as the kiss ended. "Thank you for doing what I couldn't do. I needed to talk to Mel, but I was weak."

"You were too close to her. I had to be the one to do it. We had a good talk. We've had several since then, actually."

Mel wiped her eyes. "Yeah, we're BFFs now. So watch out. We might gang up to keep you in line."

"I welcome the challenge." Sam grinned. "I'm actually thrilled to see you two getting along. It's been a while coming."

Kim and Dave stepped forward for hugs and congratulations all around. "And now we're all going to Mario's Pizza, Levi's favorite restaurant, to celebrate," she announced. "After that, we'll take him home with us so you two can have your own private celebration."

Sam's grin widened. "Grandparents are the bomb."

* * * *

Travis opened the front door on a Sunday morning, a few weeks later, to find a very shaken Melanie on the porch. "Mel! What's wrong?" He reached for her arm. "Come in. Are you okay? Are you sick?"

"Yes. No. I don't know." She grasped his arm and clung to it.

Sam joined them. "Hey, Mel! What are you doing here? You hungry? Trav makes kick-ass pancakes on Sundays. After his hour-long bike ride, that is. He keeps suggesting we go with him, but so far I've held him off."

Travis smiled. "Wait till I get you and Levi those new bikes we talked about. Then you'll have no choice." He turned back to Mel. "Are you hungry?"

She waved a hand then pressed it to her stomach. "No thanks. I need to sit down."

Travis led her to the sofa and sat down next to her. He glanced at Sam. "Where's Levi?"

"He went to get dressed, but I hear him playing with toys in his room. We've got a few minutes." He sat on the other side of Mel. "What's going on?"

Tears preceded her words. "Oh, God. I can't believe it. Just when I was starting to get my act together."

Travis' heart fluttered. "Did you relapse?"

"No, but thanks for going there first. I guess I'm always going to get that, aren't I?"

Sam frowned. "Then *what is it*?"

She looked at him and whispered, "I'm pregnant."

"Oh my God." Sam gave her a hug. "Have you —?"

"No." She shook her head firmly. "I haven't been with anyone since that night."

"The night you were attacked," he confirmed.

Travis' mind raced as he stood and walked the floor.

"Attacked isn't exactly the right word," she said. "But for lack of a better one, yeah. Damn it! Things were really looking up for me, too. I've been to Eddie's shop a few times, and that was going well. He's such a sweet man. God, what's he going to think of me?"

Sam looked at her. "Are you considering having it?"

She gaped at him. "Seriously? What choice do I have?"

"Well, there's always —"

"I could *never* have an abortion," she cut him off.

Travis smiled at the way they finished each other's sentences. Then his mind went back to the problem at hand.

Mel continued, "I know lots of people do it, and maybe in a less clear-headed state, I might have considered it back in the day. But right here and now, I don't think it's an option. I've got to have it, and just hope there's somebody decent out there, somewhere, who'll want my baby."

Travis stopped pacing. "There is."

Sam and Mel looked at him.

He felt giddy, like Scrooge on Christmas morning. Travis knew he probably looked just as nutso as Scrooge had to the townspeople. He fought the urge to dance with glee like the old man had. "We want it."

Sam blinked. "Excuse me?"

Mel said, "What?"

Travis knelt in front of her. "If you're going to have the baby anyway, then why can't Sam and I have it? He or she will be Levi's sibling, after all." He glanced at Sam. "We may never get another opportunity like this one."

"An opportunity?" Sam repeated, still stunned.

Mel smiled. "Are you serious? Because that would be an answer to my prayers."

"Hell yes, I'm serious! *A baby*. A sweet little newborn. That would be an answer to many people's prayers. We'd be honored if you'd give us the privilege of taking him or her."

Mel threw her arms around his neck and hugged him tight.

Travis laughed and wiped her tears, then they held hands for a minute and grinned at each other.

Sam said, "We don't know anything about the father, other than he was a drug-using scumbag. Do we even know what color he is?"

Travis frowned at Sam. "Does that matter? I'd welcome any color of child, as I'm sure about a million other parents would, too."

Sam waved a hand. "No, the color doesn't matter. I'm just trying to process. This makes the second time you two have added a child to our family without consulting me, and I need a minute to wrap my head around it."

Chuckling, Travis drew Sam into a hug. "I know. I'm sorry. What can I say? I love surprises. But you're right, I should have spoken with you about adopting Levi before I broached the subject with Mel *or* him. It's just that I *knew* how you felt. I already knew what your answer would be."

"Okay, but sometimes a guy needs to be asked the question. Such as, 'do you want to raise a newborn baby, Sam?' Because if you recall, you go to work every day, Dr. Nelson. That leaves me and the kiddo here all alone. Diapers, formula, spit up, colic, teething, diaper rash…"

Travis grinned. "Doesn't that sound amazing?"

Sam groaned. "And naps. There'd better be a fucking large number of naps."

Mel smiled. "Babies usually nap, Sammy, but you can't count on it."

"I'm not talking about the baby. The naps will be for me."

"You can have all the naps you want, love." Travis kissed his temple. "And how about a nanny for the hours you're working each day? Or we can take the baby to daycare, but a nanny would be more convenient and easier to supervise."

Mel chuckled. "I pity that nanny already. She'll need a high grade security clearance before you'll leave your child alone with her, won't she?"

"Damn straight," Travis agreed. He wiggled Sam's shoulders. "What do you say, babe?"

"I don't know. Both of the kid's parents were drug users. Isn't that asking for trouble right from the get-go?"

"Look at it this way. The mother has been clean since the moment the child was conceived. She'll get the best prenatal care possible. We'll be there for her every step of the way. I think it'll be amazing to watch her progress as she grows and changes."

Mel nodded. "You've actually got me excited about it. An hour ago I felt lost and alone. Now, thanks to you, I feel like I'm part of something terrific."

"You are!" Travis squeezed her hand. "Sam, the baby's going to have your DNA, just like Levi. I don't think we could ask for a better gift."

"Babies smell so good," Mel teased.

"Not all the time," Sam reminded. "Okay, what the hell? I'm still not so sure, but I guess you two have nine months to convince me this is a great idea."

Mel touched her stomach. "Well, eight months. Seven and a half, really."

Sam groaned and closed his eyes.

* * * *

Travis and Sam made arrangements for a beach wedding at a posh resort on the shores of Lake Michigan. They chose early September over the long Labor Day weekend for the Saturday evening service. The minister was a woman recommended to them by Colt Crawford, who they'd finally gotten together with for dinner. His partner Rod was a nice guy, and they'd all enjoyed their time together. They'd had Colt and Rod to their house a couple times after, and Levi got a kick out of seeing his teacher again.

Travis and Sam had reserved a room at the resort for their honeymoon night, and they dressed there before the ceremony.

"You're sure about the 'no tie' thing?" Kim asked as she straightened the collar of Travis' white, button down shirt.

Dave added, "I brought a couple in case you changed your minds."

Travis looked at Sam, gorgeous in his black slacks with the white shirt hanging loose over it. "Nope. We're good. We plan to lose our shoes once we're on the beach, too."

"No shoes!" Levi hopped up and down. He started to take his off.

"Not yet," Sam corralled him. "You need to wear them down to the beach. We'll take them off when we get there."

"Boutonniere time." Kim pulled out a box of flowers and pinned a single red rose bud to each of the men's shirts, Levi included. "Father of the groom." She pinned one to Dave's similar white shirt. "Where's Alex? He should be here."

"I'm here!" Travis' friend came out of the bathroom. "Trying to do something with my hair. It's windy out there."

She pinned the rose bud on his white shirt.

Travis ran a hand through Alex's thick brown locks. "If it's windy, then you don't need to worry about it anyway. But you look fine."

His handsome friend smiled. "So do you! Damn, now I'm wondering why I ever let you go."

"Because you were headed to law school and I went to med school in a different state, remember? We could never have managed a long distance relationship. The college fling had to end."

"Yet we both ended up back here at home."

"But time marches on, and that other ship had sailed. We're better as friends than we ever were as"—he glanced down at Levi—"anything else. Thanks for being my best man, Alex." Travis straightened his friend's boutonniere and stepped back.

Sam wrapped his arms around Travis from behind. "Yeah, thanks, Alex. For not going to med school, mainly." He grinned.

Alex laughed. "You're welcome. I may be the best man, but you're obviously the *best man*." He winked.

Travis spun around to face him. "Yes, you are." He placed a light kiss on Sam's mouth.

"This one is marked 'minister'," Kim pulled out another flower arrangement.

Dragging himself away from his groom, Travis looked in the box. There were three wrist corsages left. "Yes, that's for Cheyanne. This one is for you, Mom." He fastened the red and white flowers around her wrist and kissed her cheek. "This last one is for Mel."

"Mommy!" Levi called.

"Be right out," Mel hollered back. She entered from another adjoining bathroom. "I have to pee, like, every five minutes."

Kim put the corsage on her wrist and straightened Mel's tight, white dress. "Oh my. Have you gained a little since we picked this out?"

"Mother!" Travis teased. The news wasn't out yet, and he didn't want anything to spoil his after-ceremony surprise.

She tugged at the top of Mel's low cut, strapless dress. "I'm just sayin'. I don't remember your chest being this big when we bought this dress."

Mel grinned and let Kim fawn over her. "Must be all that good halfway house food."

"Must be," Kim mused thoughtfully.

Dave looked around. "Are we ready? It's nice and cool in here, but your guests are probably baking out there in the sun."

Travis looked at Sam. "I'm ready. How about you?"

"Way past ready." He grinned, and glanced down at Levi. "You ready, son?"

"I don't have the rings!" Levi panicked.

"I have them." Travis patted his chest pocket. "I'll give them to you right before we start."

"I can hold them now," he insisted.

"It's a long way from here down to the beach. I don't plan on retracing our steps looking for them. No thanks, my way is fine."

Sam smiled at Levi. "Something to keep in mind for future reference, kiddo. Daddy Travis' way is usually the best way."

Travis slipped a finger through one of Sam's belt loops. "Don't knock my choices, babe. You're one of them." He winked.

"Let's go!" Dave ushered them out.

Travis and Sam each took one of Levi's hands, and they all walked down to the beach. When they reached the sand, everyone kicked off their shoes and lined them up with all the guests'. Travis tucked the wedding rings into Levi's pants pocket.

Kim gave the last wrist corsage to the smiling black minister in a flowing purple dress. The woman took her place at the front of the crowd of one hundred people or so. The rows of white chairs were divided by a center aisle.

Dave turned on the CD player, and Israel Kamakawiwo'ole's version of *Over the Rainbow* began playing. The guests rose and faced the back.

Mel and Alex walked down the aisle together.

Sam and Travis followed, still holding Levi's hands as he walked between them. Travis smiled at his friends as he passed them, his nurses, a couple of the doctors in his practice, Eddie, Colt and Rod. They reached the front and Mel stepped in to take Levi's hand. She led him off to the side.

Travis closed ranks with Sam and they gazed at each other lovingly.

Dave paused the music.

Cheyanne began, "Welcome, friends, to the wedding of Sam Madison and Travis Nelson. To begin, the grooms have chosen a passage called *Apache Wedding Blessing, an Indian Marriage Prayer.*"

She gazed at each of the grooms. "Now you will feel no rain, for each of you will be shelter for the other. Now you will feel no cold, for each of you will be warmth for the other. Now there is no more loneliness. Now you are two persons but there is only one life before you. May your days together be good and long upon the Earth."

She instructed, "Travis and Sam, please face each other, join hands, and say the vows you've chosen."

Travis turned to his handsome groom and his heart swelled with love. He reached for Sam's hand and held it. "I, Travis, take you, Sam, to be my husband. I promise to be true to you in good times and in bad, in sickness and in health. I will love you and honor you all the days of my life."

Eyes glowing, Sam repeated the vows. "I, Sam, take you, Travis, to be my husband. I promise to be true to you in good times and in bad, in sickness and in health. I will love you and honor you all the days of my life."

Cheyanne asked, "Do we have the rings?"

Levi stepped forward and handed her the two bands.

She smiled and nodded to him. "The wedding ring is the outward and visible sign of an inward and spiritual bond that unites two hearts in love. It is a seal of the vows Travis and Sam have made to one another. Bless these rings, that Sam and Travis, who give them, and who wear them, may ever abide in peace. Living together in unity, love and happiness for the rest of their lives." She held her hand out.

Travis took Sam's ring and slipped it on his lover's finger. "Sam, I give you this ring to wear with love and joy. As this ring has no end, neither shall my love for you. I choose you to be my husband this day."

Sam took Travis' ring from the minister and slid it on Trav's finger. "This ring I give you as a token of my abiding love and true devotion. With my heart I pledge to you all that I am. And with this ring I marry you to join my life to yours."

Cheyanne said, "Nourished by understanding, warmed by friends, fed by loved ones, matured by wisdom. Tempered by tears, made holy by caring and sharing. Be blessed always. Go forth in peace! But first, you may kiss your groom."

Smiling, Travis and Sam shared a tender kiss.

The crowd cheered, and Levi tugged at each of their pant legs as he hopped up and down.

"I now pronounce you, husband and husband!" Cheyanne waved her hands over them.

Dave hit the CD player again, and Bobby McFerrin's *Don't Worry, Be Happy* started playing. Travis, Sam and Levi walked back down the aisle as the guests blew bubbles in their direction.

The reception flew by like a blur in Travis' mind. They cut the cake and sipped champagne on the beach. Music played, people danced, and drinks flowed. By the time darkness fell and the bamboo torches were lit, there were just a few close friends and family left celebrating.

Travis chose that time to make his announcement. With him and Sam flanking Mel, and holding Levi in his other arm, he said, "We'd like you to share in our good news. Most of you know that we'll be filing papers this week to begin the formal adoption process with Levi. Thanks, Alex." He nodded to his friend who was handling the details. "But you probably *don't* know that Melanie hasn't just been eating too much good food." He glanced at Levi then placed a hand on her stomach. "Mommy's going to have a baby. And next

March, when he or she is born, Sam and I and Levi will welcome the new baby into our family."

Gasps of surprised ran through the crowd. Kim nodded knowingly and hugged her husband. Levi stared back and forth from his dads to his mom. "A baby?"

"Isn't that exciting?" Sam prompted.

"Cool!" Levi shouted, and scooted out of Travis' arms to hug his mother.

The photographer took hundreds of shots, but none more precious to Travis than the image of Levi kissing his mother's little baby bump. He squeezed Sam's hand and the two of them joined Levi to kiss her stomach, too.

* * * *

Late that night, as he lay in his husband's arms, Travis mused about their perfect day. "The wind simply stopped blowing, like that was the plan all along."

"The temperature was perfect. September was a great choice," Sam agreed.

"*You* were a great choice." Travis kissed his neck. "The champagne, maybe not so much. For a while there I was afraid it might knock me on my ass."

"You rebounded." Sam patted the aforementioned body part. "And rebounded again."

Travis stretched. "I'm fixing to rebound again. I wanna make love to you all night long. We can sleep when we're dead. Tonight is about you and me, sharing our love."

"Now you will feel no cold, for each of you will be warmth for the other," Sam repeated a line from their ceremony.

Travis rubbed their noses together. "Living together in unity, love and happiness for the rest of our lives."

"Oh yeah." Sam reached for his husband's shaft and squeezed it. "Starting with right now." Their kiss became passion-fueled and soon they were joined and rocking together again.

In a white-hot frenzy, Travis climaxed again and again as they kept going through the night. He remembered looking at the clock somewhere around five a.m. Sam had just dozed off. Satisfied that he'd fulfilled his promise, Travis smiled and closed his eyes.

* * * *

Travis was seeing patients a few weeks later when he received a call from Alex on his cell. "Hey, buddy, I just have a couple of minutes. The office is packed with sick little'uns."

"Travis, who is James Fielding?"

He searched his brain but couldn't come up with the name. "No idea. Why?"

"I told you we had to publish the legal notice of intent to adopt in the newspaper three times."

"Sure." For some reason, a feeling of dread oozed through his system.

"Apparently, Mr. Fielding saw it."

"Lots of people probably saw it. I doubt most of them cared."

"Most of them probably didn't. Fielding evidently cared. He and his wife Marianne have filed a petition to block the adoption."

Travis' heart leaped into his throat. "They what?"

"They're suing for custody of Levi."

Chapter Twelve

Sam fidgeted uncomfortably in the overstuffed chair in Alex West's law office. When he'd phoned Mel he'd known it would take her an hour to get there. He and Travis had each arrived within thirty minutes, and the wait after that was tense.

"My mom is getting Levi, then?" Travis asked for the third time.

"Yes. I spoke with her twice. She won't have a problem getting there in time."

"Thanks." He paced around the large office, as he usually did. Travis could not sit still when he was worried.

"You could tell me what you know about the Fieldings," Alex suggested to Sam.

"Not much. I may have met them once. I seem to recall Mel saying they were homophobic and very religious."

"Great. We're off to a good start then, with two gay defendants and a gay lawyer."

Sam and Travis looked at each other with panic in their eyes. "Do we need to find a different lawyer?" Sam wondered aloud.

Alex folded his arms across his broad chest. "Are you going to find different defendants, too?"

"Of course not."

The lawyer smiled. "Then give me a chance. There's not much I enjoy more than ripping people like them to shreds."

Travis frowned. "I don't get it. In all these months that we've been together, I've not heard about these people. No phone calls to Levi, or inquiring about him. Holidays have come and gone, school programs, all that shit. Never a mention of them. Now all of a sudden they show up demanding custody?"

The door opened and Alex's secretary showed Mel in.

She looked as drawn and nervous as Sam felt.

"Hey." He jumped up and kissed her cheek, then offered her his chair. He chose a different one, and they all sat.

"This is bullshit," she commented.

Alex replied, "I just asked Sam to tell me what he knows about the Fieldings, which was not much. Tell me what you know."

She shook her head. "They're strange rangers. Pretty religious, I know they used to go to church more than once a week. I remember when Rob got his first tattoo, his mother didn't speak to him for a month. I thought it was a blessing, but he didn't think that was funny. She eventually came around."

Alex glanced at Travis. "Doesn't like tattoos. Something else we have going for us."

"No shit. Mel, when's the last time you heard from them? Sam can't remember any recent contact."

"In person, it was before Rob was arrested. The last time I saw them was at his sentencing." She looked at Alex. "Rob signed away his parental rights. His lawyer said he had no chance of parole before Levi turns eighteen, and it was in Levi's best interests to sign rights to me so I could make all the legal decisions for him. So he did. His grandparents have no claim on him, right?"

"In Illinois, grandparents do have rights, but very rarely are they held in higher esteem than parental rights. The issue here is sticky, though, since you're effectively signing away your parental rights. So now it's uncle versus grandparents."

"But I'm still in the picture. It's not like I'm just giving him away. Doesn't what I want carry any weight? And, more importantly, doesn't what *Levi* wants matter the most?"

"It matters, but I won't say it's the most important factor. Some children aren't able to make informed, intelligent decisions for themselves. Levi is, of course, and hopefully when the judge talks to him, he or she will see that for herself."

"The judge will talk to him?" Travis repeated. He looked so upset, Sam's heart felt like it was breaking.

"Yes. But first, we'll have a hearing in front of the judge to determine if the case has any merit, and should go forward. They could toss it out right then, but I doubt they will. We'll probably go to trial, so we'll need to provide character witnesses for the two of you. Your parents should try to be there, they'll look good sitting in the gallery."

"Trial," Travis said, his eyes glassy.

"Come on now, I believe we have a good shot. A lot depends on which judge we get. Gay adoptions are legal here, and being gay is a protected class in discrimination lawsuits."

"What does that mean, exactly?" Sam asked.

"Put simply, it means that no one can discriminate against you for being gay, any more than they can discriminate against a woman or a black person. Now, having said that, there are still a few judges out there who are old school. They think marriage should be between one man and one woman, regardless of what the Illinois Supreme Court said. If we land one of them, we'll have a tougher time making our case."

"This is horrible!" Travis waved his hands. "I had no idea anything like this could happen. I should never have brought up the adoption issue."

"Don't panic," Alex advised. "If we get a bad feeling as we go along, Mel might be able to withdraw her consent. You won't be Levi's legal parents, but he could still live with you. That's our last resort."

Sam had to ask. "You said Mel *might* be about to withdraw her consent? Why wouldn't she be able to?"

Alex winced. "If the judge wants to play hardball, he or she could refuse her petition. The case would have to go forward with them ruling in favor of either you two, or the Fieldings."

"Oh my God." Travis put his face in his hands. "We could lose him."

Sam rose and went to stand by his husband, placing a hand on his back. "Don't think like that. We've got a good shot, Alex said."

The lawyer nodded. "I really think we do. Start making a list of witnesses you could call. Teachers, family friends, anyone who's seen you with Levi and knows how well the boy is doing in your care."

"We can do that," Sam agreed.

Alex looked at Mel. "Anything else you can think of to tell me about the Fieldings?"

She thought about it. "They used to private message me on Facebook. I wouldn't accept their friend requests, but they kept sending me messages, asking to see pictures of Levi. They tagged themselves in one of his photos. I removed the tags and stopped posting his picture online."

"Good." Alex jotted notes. "Facebook stalking. We might be able to use it. Anything else?"

Mel shook her head.

"Keep thinking. We need every shred of evidence we can get on these people, the dirtier the better. Let me know if you come up with anything."

"I will."

Alex stood and saw them out. "Keep a positive attitude." He clasped Travis' shoulder. "You hear me? Think positive. We're four strong people against two cowardly zealots. We can do this. We *will* do this."

Travis nodded, and Sam walked him out. "Thanks." He smiled at Alex.

"I'll be in touch soon."

Sam stood with his family next to their cars in the parking lot. "This is totally unbelievable."

Travis ran his hands through his hair. "I feel like shit. I can't believe this is going down."

"Take it easy," Sam squeezed his hands. "Go home and try to unwind. Go for a bike ride, maybe. I'll go get Levi and be there soon." He looked at Mel. "Would you like to come for dinner?"

She shook her head. "No, but thanks. I'm meeting Eddie later to go over some designs."

Sam groaned. "He didn't say anything about showing you his etchings, did he?"

"Huh?"

He grinned. "Never mind. Be careful. We'll talk to you soon."

Mel drove off, but Travis sat frozen behind his steering wheel.

"Hey, ready to go?" Sam tried to sound cheerful.

"Oh God, Sam! What have I done?" Travis broke down, his shoulders shaking as he cried.

"Hey, hey. Come on, now. You didn't do anything. This is all going to be okay. You told me Alex is a great lawyer." He held Travis and let him sob into Sam's shoulder.

"What if we lose him to people Levi doesn't even know? What kind of life will he have with them? God, Sam, I'm petrified for him."

Sam spoke quietly into his ear. "You can share any thought you have with me. Any time. But when you're with Levi, you will *not* talk to him like this. We don't even want to mention this to him until we have to. He'll be frightened, and if he sees how scared you are, it will devastate him. Do you hear me?"

Travis nodded.

"Think positive thoughts."

"Positive thoughts," Travis repeated, and broke down again. Sam held him, and let him cry.

* * * *

Sam didn't own a suit, but wore one of Travis' jackets to the first, informal hearing with the judge and the Fieldings present. A basket-case on the inside, he thought he appeared fairly calm and collected on the outside.

Travis had pulled himself together, too. They'd had several meetings with Alex and were all prepared for how the hearing would run.

Mel met them at the courthouse, and they all walked in together.

The Fieldings and their lawyer sat at a table on the left side of the room. Alex led them to the table on the right, and they took their seats.

Sam studied Rob's parents. James was probably fifty, with salt and pepper colored hair. His jacket was tan corduroy, and he didn't look that comfortable in it.

Marianne had a silver, shoulder-length bob haircut. Her face had a nasty expression on it already. Sam realized she was watching him as he checked her out, and he looked away quickly.

"All rise," the bailiff announced, and they stood. "Court is now in session. The honorable Judge Marsha Needham presiding."

A short, squat and wide black woman in a long black robe entered and took her seat behind the bench. Sam couldn't get a read on her expression. He wondered what Alex was thinking about the judge they'd drawn.

Judge Needham picked up a stack of papers. "This hearing is to determine if there is just cause for a custody determination in the case of Levi Aaron Madison. James and Marianne Fielding have filed a petition, as paternal grandparents, for custody. On the other side we have Melanie Madison, the child's mother, and Sam Madison, the child's uncle. Mr. Madison and his legal husband Dr. Travis Nelson have also filed a petition for custody, with the mother's consent. Do I have all that right?" She looked at Alex.

He stood. "Yes, Your Honor. I might mention that Mr. Madison and Dr. Nelson filed their petition first, with the full blessing of the child's mother and the child himself."

"That's what I said, Counselor. Don't try to grandstand me. I've been on this bench longer than you've been on the Earth."

"I'm sorry, Your Honor." Alex took his seat.

She looked to the other table. "Mr. Winston, on what grounds are your clients suing for custody?"

The opposing lawyer rose. "Your Honor, my clients are good, law-abiding, church-going citizens. When they heard that the mother of their grandson was suffering from drug addiction and had to be sent to rehab, they reached out to her and offered help caring for the boy. She rebuked them because they've never had a close relationship. But now that she's apparently realized she can't care for the boy, they believe they should be the first ones considered as legal guardians. The men she's chosen have a history of poor choices which we feel would negatively impact the boy."

"What kind of choices, and do you have any proof?"

The lawyer looked down on Sam and his family. "Your Honor, the men are *gay*. We understand they have tattoos. This is not the atmosphere we'd choose to subject an impressionable six year old to, and we find their behavior completely unacceptable."

"Oh, good Lord." The judge rolled her eyes. "So your clients are the salt of the earth and these two came from Sodom and Gomorrah. I get that." She looked at Alex. "Counselor, what do you have to say for your clients before I have them thrown to the lion's den for their lewd and lascivious behavior?"

Alex rose and offered a small smile. "Your Honor. Dr. Nelson is a highly respected pediatrician with his own practice here in town. Mr. Madison is a writer who earns a very good living and both men are able to care for Levi comfortably. We have a list of people prepared to speak on their behalf, including some of Levi's teachers, one of whom can attest to the improvement in the child's hygiene and attitude when he went to live with my clients, as compared to the time that the boy lived with his parents, including the plaintiff's son. We would also like to note that Dr. Nelson's parents, both teachers themselves, have been very hands-on grandparents and a positive influence in the boy's life. And finally, Ms. Madison, Levi's mother, has completed her self-imposed rehabilitation and is now working and doing very well. It is my clients' intentions to allow her to be involved in the child's life as much as either of them wishes, as long as she remains clean and sober. Which is, of course, her plan."

"Duly noted. Okay, gentlemen. At first I didn't see a case here, but now I'm intrigued. I'd like to hear what the witnesses have to say, and I'll be speaking with Levi as well. Each of the plaintiffs and defendants should be prepared to testify. We'll begin next Monday at nine a.m. My court clerk will let you know when to bring Levi. I'll meet with him in my chambers. I don't want him in the courtroom at any time." She banged her gavel and rose.

The bailiff said, "All rise. Plaintiffs and defendants are dismissed to Monday at nine a.m."

Sam looked at Travis and Mel, and they all looked at Alex.

He sighed. "Well then. Monday at nine it is. At first, judging by her demeanor, I thought she might throw the whole thing out. She surprised me."

Sam stared at the empty judge's bench. "Surprised. Yeah. Me too."

* * * *

Travis held Levi's hand as Alex walked them back to the judge's chambers. The first day of testimony had gone pretty much as expected. He and Sam had each taken the stand and told their story. Mel had had it a little harder, as the opposing lawyer had tried to cut her down at every turn. His last question to her was if she was pregnant, and who the father of her child was.

Alex had anticipated the question, and she'd given the response they'd rehearsed. "I was inseminated. The father is Dr. Travis Nelson. He and my brother are going to adopt the baby once it's born."

Travis had been concerned about her perjuring herself, but Alex had insisted she was speaking the truth. She had been inseminated. They never used the word 'artificially'. And Travis would be the father.

Now he felt like he was walking his child down a gangplank, with alligators waiting at the other end. Travis could tell Levi was shaking. He wasn't doing much better himself.

Alex knocked on the judge's door.

A woman opened it.

"Come in," the judge called. "Levi, I'm Judge Needham. This is Mrs. Adams from the Department of Children and Family Services. She'll be sitting in on the interview today." She glanced at Travis. "You men can go, now. I'll return him to you when we're done."

Travis squeezed Levi's hand and reluctantly released it. He left with Alex, and returned to the room where Mel and Sam waited with his parents.

Half an hour later, Mrs. Adams brought Levi to them with instructions that he needed to be taken out immediately. Dave offered to drive him to school, and after hugs all around, they left.

"Court is resuming." Alex led them back into the courtroom and the trial picked up where it had left off the day before.

Kim testified on behalf of her and Dave, professing their love for Levi.

Colt expressed the concerns he'd had about Levi when he was under the care of his parents, and explained how the situation had turned around once Sam and Travis had taken responsibility for him.

Their final witness was Mrs. Lamb, Levi's current teacher. She was sworn in and Alex asked her a few questions. She had nothing but a glowing report of the boy and his supportive family.

"Mrs. Lamb," Alex asked his final question, "have you ever seen Levi's grandparents at his school for any event?"

"Oh goodness, yes. They're there for *every* event and program. Levi raves about them. He obviously loves them very much."

Alex pointed to the Fieldings. "These grandparents, Mrs. Lamb? James and Marianne Fielding?"

She looked confused. "No, I've never seen those people before. I meant those grandparents." She pointed to Kim in the gallery. "Mr. and Mrs. Nelson. They love Levi so much."

Alex turned to the judge. "Nothing further, Your Honor."

The judge turned to the Fielding's lawyer. "Anything, Mr. Winston?"

"No, Your Honor."

She dismissed Mrs. Lamb then turned back to Winston. "Would one of your clients like to make a final plea?"

Mrs. Fielding rose. "Your Honor, I'm sure anyone could dredge up a few people to come in and attest to their fitness as a parent. It's obvious that's what these men have done. And there's no doubt the boy's life is better now than it was before, when he was living with a drug-addicted mother. But just because something is *better* doesn't make it good, or right. We are God-fearing, bible-reading Christians who firmly believe that homosexuality is wrong. And exposing that boy to their influence is dooming him to a life of full of sin and earthly temptations. It's wrong in God's eyes, and it's wrong in our eyes. It's simply unacceptable. We long to give the boy a proper home and raise him in a loving, Christian family. That's all we want. We have the boy's best interests at heart." She looked down demurely then took her seat.

Travis clenched and unclenched his fists. He turned to Sam and whispered, "You want this? Because if not, I've got it."

"If you know what you're going to say then by all means, go for it." Sam squeezed his arm.

The judge looked at Alex. "Mr. West? Who's going to speak for the defendants?"

Travis rose. "I am, Your Honor. I guess this all boils down to my husband and I believing in a very different God than Mrs. Fielding described. We're Christians as well, but we don't fear the Lord, we embrace him. And he embraces our family every day of our lives. There's nothing I can say to bigots who believe that homosexuality is a sin and I'm not going to debate that today. All I can tell you is that our household is filled with love, respect and support for one another. There's nothing sinful, and we don't have any more or less temptations than heterosexual people do. Melanie Madison has worked very hard to overcome her addictions and we're blessed to have her in our lives. We support her efforts and feel that Levi's life is enriched by having his mother close to him. We've surrounded him with loving, non-judgmental grandparents and friends who give us as much love and support to us as we do to them. If there's been any unacceptable behavior brought to light here today, I trust you can see which table it's coming from. And as for having *the boy's* best interests at heart, well…" He looked at the Fieldings. "His name is Levi. I've yet to hear you use it. And I don't see how someone who hasn't spent five minutes alone with him in the past year or longer could really know what his best interests are." He placed a hand over his heart, and turned back to the judge. "I know Levi. Sam knows Levi. And of course, his mother knows him well enough to understand that we can provide some of the things she can't right now. Make no mistake about it, she's not giving him up. She's doing her best to make his life better. I love her for that. Sam loves her because she's his twin sister and they have that kind of bond. Not having any siblings, it took me a while to figure that out. But I get it now, and I want that for my son. Levi is excited to have a brother or sister in the spring. Our family will be complete. We're all looking forward to it." He choked up. "Please don't tear apart my family." Travis sat down quickly, forcing back the tears.

Sam wrapped his arms around Travis and pressed his forehead against Trav's temple.

The judge studied them for a moment, then collected her thoughts before she spoke. "Typically I would adjourn court and take a few days to make my ruling. I'm not going to do that to this family. I've put you through enough. I regret that I had to do it, but I was really interested to see if Mr. and Mrs. Fielding had any basis for their case other than pure hate and bigotry. I was sadly disappointed to discover they didn't."

She looked at the Fieldings. "Sir and Madam, you may come from a God-fearing, bible-thumping home, but that didn't keep your son from selling drugs and ending up in prison for an extended amount of time, did it? I get the feeling you were looking for a do-over with your grandson and, folks, it just doesn't work that way. The half hour I spent with Levi showed me what an intelligent, perceptive child he is. Growing up in the home where he is now, I can only imagine how empathetic and compassionate he'll be as he gets older. The world needs more people like that, and I applaud these young people for wanting to provide that to their children. And personally, I'd rather pray to their God than yours, any day of the week."

Travis and Sam exchanged hopeful glances. Alex gripped one of Travis' hands under the table and they all held their breath.

"I'm hereby ruling in favor of the defendants in this case, and the petition for adoption by Dr. Travis Nelson and Mr. Sam Madison has been granted. There's a six month waiting period during which time you'll have to pass an inspection by the department of Children and Family Services, but I have no doubts you'll breeze through that. The name change has been granted effective immediately, and your son is now Levi Aaron Madison-Nelson. Normally I would suggest that the parents be considerate toward the grandparents and offer them visitation. But in this case, gentlemen, I don't blame you for keeping your son as far away as possible from such hateful, ignorant bigots. Court is dismissed." She banged her gavel and stood, then reconsidered and looked back at the shocked Fieldings. "And by the way, I'd show you my tattoo if it was in a place that I could do so with decency. But it's not, so I won't." She nodded her head and walked out.

Travis and Sam laughed, and soon everyone was hugging everyone else. It took Travis a minute to realize that Alex had removed his suit coat and was rolling up his sleeves so his tattooed arms were visible. Travis grinned and did the same thing.

When he turned around, he laughed, realizing Colt and Eddie had both done it as well.

The Fieldings and their lawyer pushed past them with shocked expressions as they stomped out.

Sam called, "If *my* chattoo was in a place I could show you with decency I would. But I can't, so I won't."

His family laughed as they gathered around.

Mel ran a hand over Alex's arm. "Holy guacamole! You're all marked men! You should start a club or something."

"Maybe we will," Sam teased.

Eddie chuckled. "You'd be a probationary member, plebe. One tattoo does not a 'marked man' make."

"Hey, I'm planning to get more. Lots more. My next one is going to be a sketch Mel's doing of Travis."

Eddie winced. "I don't like to tattoo significant other's faces, 'cause half the time the relationship doesn't work out."

Travis put an arm around Sam. "We're going to make it, Eddie. No worries."

Eddie leaned in to Sam. "Make sure it's a small one, just in case I have to do a cover up."

"No cover ups," Travis insisted. "We made it over this hurdle, and we'll make it over the next one." He squeezed Sam's hand. "We're stronger together than we ever were apart."

"Totally." Sam leaned in for a kiss.

As it did so often when Sam kissed him, Travis' heart soared.

Epilogue

"Breathe! Hee hee hee, hoo hoo hoo." Sam held Mel's hand as he coached her through the Lamaze childbirth technique.

She replied through gritted teeth, "Obviously I am breathing, or I'd be dead. And if you say 'hee hee hoo hoo' to me again, you might be dead, too."

He grinned. "I know you don't mean it, it's just the pain talking."

"No, I mean it." She grimaced as another contraction hit her.

Travis clasped her other hand. "The epidural should have lasted longer. It's too late to give you anything else now. You're just gonna have to tough it out, babe."

"Arrgh!" She yelled, and they both squeezed her hands.

"We're almost there, Mel." The OB doctor checked the baby's position. "One or two more good contractions and I'll have you push."

"They're all good ones!" she protested loudly, and panted through a few more.

"Here we go," the doctor agreed. "I want you to push with the next one. Tell me when you're ready."

"Now," she groaned, and pushed.

"Bear down, bear down," the doctor coached.

"That's it!" Sam watched a slimy little head appear.

"It's coming!" Travis gaped as the rest of the body popped out.

The doctor plopped the infant on Mel's stomach and picked up the scissors. "Who's going to cut the cord?"

Sam smiled at Travis. "Do it together?"

Travis nodded, and put his hand over Sam's as they snipped the child apart from its mother.

"Well?" Sam asked impatiently.

The doctor waggled his eyebrows. "It's a girl."

He gazed at Travis. "A girl!"

Travis grinned wildly. "We have a daughter." He kissed Mel's temple. "You did it. We have a daughter."

She took some deep breaths. "Can I see her?"

"Just hang on." The nurse cleaned the baby up. "One minute Apgar score is nine."

"That's good," Travis said. He went to the bassinet and supervised the team of nurses.

"What's Apgar?" a drowsy Mel asked.

Sam ticked the words off on his fingers. "Appearance, Pulse, Grimace, Activity, Respiration. The best score is ten."

"Why isn't she a ten?" Mel asked.

"Hold your horses." The nurses continued to work on her. "Five minute Apgar is ten." She brought the swaddled infant to Mel and handed her over.

"Oh, God! She's pink and perfect and beautiful. Look at all that straight, brown hair."

Sam smiled at Travis. "Just like her daddy."

Travis chuckled. "Finally. I thought I'd be surrounded by blue-eyed blonds forever."

Mel placed a light kiss on the baby's head and handed her to Sam. "Go see your daddy, sweet girl."

The doctor said, "Are you ready to deliver the placenta? This will be a breeze by comparison."

"Why not?" She took another breath and pushed to expel the afterbirth.

Sam showed the baby to Travis and they admired her together. "She's beautiful."

Travis gazed into his eyes. "You're good with this, right? I know you were hesitant at first."

Grinning, Sam turned his back. "Don't even think of taking away my baby. This is my girl. My buddy. We're gonna have so much fun."

Travis laughed and kissed his cheek.

Mel was leaning back, resting again. "Does your buddy have a name?"

Sam gazed at Travis. "We're going to call her Lilah. Lilah Renee Madison-Nelson."

A tear streamed down Mel's cheek. "Aw. Mom's name was Delilah."

Travis nodded. "And my mom's middle name is Renee. We're honoring them both."

She yawned. "You didn't want to honor the person who did all the work?"

Travis brushed back Mel's hair. "We thought about it, we really did. We just decided that might have been confusing."

Sam leaned in. "But if you really want us to, we'll call the next one you have Melanie."

Her eyes popped. "Screw you, man. First chance I get I'm having my tubes tied. Be happy with what you've got."

"We're very happy." Sam leaned down and kissed Mel's forehead.

Travis moved behind him and wrapped his arms around Sam's waist. He kissed his husband's cheek and smiled down at their sleeping daughter. "If I was any happier, I might just float away."

About the Author

Jenna Byrnes could use more cabinet space and more hours in a day. She'd fill the kitchen with gadgets her husband purchases off TV and let him cook for her to his heart's content. She'd breeze through the days adding hours of sleep, and more time for writing the hot, erotic romance she loves to read.

Jenna thinks everyone deserves a happy ending, and loves to provide as many of those as possible to her gay, lesbian and hetero characters. Her favorite quote, from a pro-gay billboard, is "Be careful who you hate. It may be someone you love."

Jenna Byrnes loves to hear from readers. You can find her contact information, website and author biography at http://pride-publishing.com.

www.ingramcontent.com/pod-product-compliance
Lightning Source LLC
Chambersburg PA
CBHW020409180626
46812CB00003B/897